The Sitka Killings

It's 1867. The USA has just purchased Alaska from the Russian Empire, and sent Colonel Jefferson Davis and part of the 9th Infantry to take possession of the 'last frontier'. Replacing the 'Russkies' would prove to be the easy part, though, and governing the new territory something else entirely, because the soldiers are barely off the steamship before two officers are brutally slain in Sitka's cathedral.

Jake Pierce is an embittered army scout, assigned to 'handle' any troublesome Indians that might be encountered. The problem is, for a man filled with hate, the only good Indian is a dead one! And that could lead him and his new partner, Cleetus Payne, into more trouble than even he can handle. Especially as they are tasked with tracking the two assassins into mainland Alaska. With the reason for the killings unclear, this proves to be only the start of something very nasty indeed!

The Sitka Killings

Paul Bedford

A Black Horse Western

ROBERT HALE

ISBN 978 0 7198 3138 6

The Crowood Press
The Stable Block
Crowood Lane
Ramsbury
Marlborough
Wiltshire SN8 2HR

www.bhwesterns.com

Robert Hale is an imprint
of The Crowood Press

In fond memory of my father, Ronald Bedford,
forever in my thoughts

CHAPTER ONE

Jake Pierce regarded the alien shoreline through sleepless and thoroughly jaundiced eyes. Seven days of abject misery on board the steam sloop USS *Ossipee* had left him drained, depressed and utterly listless. Although the fifteen-hundred-mile journey, northbound out of San Francisco, had been mercifully storm free, for a 'landlubber' used only to solid ground under his feet, the voyage had been sheer torment as seasickness quickly overwhelmed him. His innards were scarred from the continuous retching that he thought would never cease. The fact that he and many other passengers without 'sea legs' were the obvious butt of amusement for the *Ossipee*'s crew only compounded the grim experience. His condition served as an uncomfortable reminder of the terminally ill victims of yellow fever whom he had seen during the recent war against slavery, who had ended their days helplessly vomiting black bile. And yet despite all this, on each of the last three days he had doggedly made his way up on to the deck because the chill, fresh air at least gave him an illusion of well being.

As various structures came into view in the distance, the wooden naval vessel began a slow turn to starboard, trailing black smoke from its single stack. As it finally dawned on Jake's numbed wits that this had to be their destination, and that the dreadful journey was actually coming to a close, a spark of interest was abruptly ignited. He had spent his adult life in the wilder parts of the rapidly expanding United States, and never tired of new vistas. And with an abundance of timber available and snow-capped peaks majestically towering over Alaska's capital, he decided that the City of Novo Arkhangelsk, soon to be renamed Sitka, occupied an undeniably striking and practical location. Whether his time spent there would be agreeable was something else again. Although Baranof Island, upon which the community was situated, lay at the western edge of the Alaska panhandle, well south of the bulk of the vast and mostly unexplored territory, the winters would still be far colder than any he had grown used to of late.

The ship's speed began to ease off as they drew closer, and Jake was soon able to make out the buildings in far greater detail. Bordering the impressive natural harbour were a great many wooden cabins, but off to the left, atop what appeared to be a natural hill, was an imposing two-storey brick building boasting a cupola on its roof. And from a flagpole in front of it, flew the undeniably stirring eagle flag of the Russian Empire, its martial presence reinforced by the gaping muzzles of a number of large cannon. Despite his aching guts, the American chuckled. Oh, they had definitely arrived all right!

As if confirming that thought, a hive of activity broke out on deck. The sloop's crew of one hundred and forty-one officers and men was rapidly outnumbered as blue-coated infantry ascended from the cramped and gloomy confines below. Non-coms bawled at them to 'fix themselves' and show a little military spirit, which wasn't easy when many of them were in a far worse condition than Jake. Then Major Edwin Thomas appeared, and he winked at the lone civilian.

'Prefer it up here away from us blue bellies, don't you, Mister Pierce?'

Jake favoured the mild-mannered officer with a wry smile. 'The deck moves about just as much up here, but at least the air is fresher.'

Before Thomas could respond to that, if indeed he was even going to, their attention was taken by activity at the forward companionway, and three men appeared in well-tailored uniforms. As they moved over to the gunwale, a full 'bird' colonel, going by the unlikely name of Jefferson C. Davis, produced a drawtube spyglass and began a close scrutiny of the other craft anchored in the bay. In addition to the various nondescript trading vessels, there was a sizeable steamship with the name *Politkofsky* emblazoned across the stern. The officer grunted. That sure as hell didn't form any part of the United States Navy!

Although his name was *almost* identical to that of the former president of the defeated Confederacy, the colonel bore neither a physical resemblance to that man nor shared his political convictions. Heavily bearded, with pronounced bags under rather sad eyes, the prematurely aged thirty-nine-year-old Union war veteran gestured to his nearest companion and passed over the spyglass. That individual, a generously moustachioed major general in full dress uniform, immediately focused on the Russian flag ashore and also grunted.

'One thing's for sure, that thing won't be up there for much longer.'

*

As the ship's longboats crammed with soldiers approached the shore, their Russian counterparts, clothed in greatcoats to ward off the cold and with fixed bayonets, assembled to receive them. And yet there was something very unusual about this particular 'invasion'. Although the *Ossipee*'s varied selection of main armament was manned, none of the thirteen smoothbores and rifled cannon was loaded with shot, only black powder. And even a cynical cuss like Jake Pierce recognized that something pretty darned amazing – and bewildering – was unfolding in that remote spot. Because it wasn't often that a vast country changed ownership without a shot being fired in anger, although such an occurrence was not without precedent in the case of the United States. The Louisiana Purchase, some sixty-four years earlier, had been a remarkable achievement by Thomas Jefferson. Whether the blessed condition of tranquillity would continue did of course depend on how the new administration coped with its unfamiliar subjects. And Colonel Davis was not known for either tact or timidity!

*

All had soon become clear, even to those lower orders without prior knowledge of their reason for being there. The high ground was known as Castle Hill, and the brick building atop it served as the governor's residence, soon to be occupied by Colonel Davis. The parade ground in front, complete with its defensive cannon, was quickly filled by two hundred and fifty men of the US 9th Infantry and eighty unexceptional-looking Russian soldiers. The colonel had no particulars of their history and even less interest. He just wanted them and their garishly attired masters gone from the United States' most recent purchase.

Whether the vast territory was a bargain at seven million dollars plus change also didn't concern him. Davis had been assigned the task of administering it as the military Department of Alaska, and that was exactly what he would do. But for that to happen, the Russian Eagle first had to be lowered, in a somewhat stilted handover ceremony, so allowing the officials their brief moment in the limelight. It was Friday 18 October 1867, and in that part of the globe the world was definitely turning. Probably a great deal faster than most of them realized, because the change of ownership had also meant a shift from the Julian to the Gregorian calendar. This had resulted in the bizarre situation of the previous day also being a Friday, and the 6 October at that!

The American Commissioner, Major General Lovell Rousseau, and his Russian counterpart, naval Captain Alexis Pestchouroff, stood with the outgoing governor and his wife, Prince and Princess Maksutov. She was a comely, well-endowed lady adorned in expensive furs, who bizarrely carried an open parasol against the non-existent sunshine. It was not to remain in her grip for long, however. In a scene of increasing desperation, it took three attempts yanking on the stubborn halyard to lower the entangled Russian flag, and then, as her nation's standard was finally released from its bonds on the flagstaff, a gust of wind ominously kicked up, tearing it from the luckless officer's grasp. The fine standard flew unerringly towards the Russian ranks and deposited itself on their upturned bayonets.

The grim symbolism representing her country's possible future destiny was obviously too much for the highly strung princess. '*Bozhe moy!*' she wailed before collapsing theatrically into her husband's arms in a dead faint. Amazingly, this farcical turn of events was received with disciplined silence by everyone... with a sole exception.

'Haw, haw, haw,' Jake Pierce guffawed from the rear of the American contingent. Back on terra firma, his spirits were returning, along with his irreverent sense of humour. 'I reckon the little lady's stays must be a mite too tight,' he remarked to anyone who might be listening.

If any Russians heard him they showed no signs of understanding, but Davis sure did. He glowered balefully over at the tall frontiersman, before remarking to Major Thomas: 'I don't like that uncouth ruffian, Major. He's altogether far too... independent.'

The other man shrugged. 'Maybe so, sir, but you just might need him. Who knows what we might come up against out here in this God-forsaken wilderness.'

They were both silenced by an angry glance from General Rousseau, who required that all attention should focus on the momentous raising of the American flag. He had travelled a long way to witness the event at the behest of Secretary of State William Seward, and fully intended to enjoy it.

Still sporting a broad grin, Jake turned away from the ceremony and sidled over to the low wall surrounding the parade ground. As he gazed down upon Sitka's rough and ready streets, the humour gradually drained from his weathered features. It occurred to him that Alaska's new masters probably didn't know anything at all about its existing inhabitants. Sure, there were the expected Russian fur traders and merchants, but that was only part of it. What about the indigenous residents who had presumably been subjugated by them? If indeed they even had. Perhaps the Russian Empire's mandate had only reached as far as the terrain covered by its guns on Castle Hill. Unknown to him, his expression had turned truly grim at the thought of encountering Indians in some form or other.

There was also another consideration. Jake knew all too well how rough and ready American frontier life could be. Surely it wouldn't be long before the soldiers of the newly arrived garrison, currently on their best behaviour, began to upset people. And it was also only a matter of time before speculators from the south arrived to claim that which they considered to be theirs by right.

His thoughtful scrutiny drifted on to a substantial building a short distance away. Constructed from logs faced with clapboard, and with roofs of wood shingle, it possessed an impressive central dome and behind it a high belltower on top of which sat a cross, thereby instantly marking it out as a place of worship. Some form of religion had obviously been a part of life in Sitka, but that was not always a good thing, especially if it had been forcibly imposed on others.

Unseen by Jake, the Stars and Stripes had been raised without hindrance, and his ruminations were abruptly shattered by the tremendous crash of the Russian smoothbores discharging around the perimeter. He couldn't imagine what *they* had to celebrate, unless it was the sale of a troublesome colony. The repeated detonations made his head hurt, and he quickly put both hands up to protect his eardrums from the brutal assault. Then, as the guns finally and mercifully fell silent and great clouds of acrid smoke blew away on the wind, the assembled soldiery let rip with orchestrated cheers. These were followed by an answering discharge of the *Ossipee*'s ordnance out in the bay.

'Christ almighty, someone's sure happy about something,' Jake muttered ruefully, before suddenly discovering Major Thomas at his shoulder.

'A word to the wise, Mister Pierce,' that man softly remarked. 'You'd be well advised not to get on the colonel's wrong side. He has a temper. Once killed a superior officer stone dead and got clean away with it. He ain't someone to mess with.'

Jake's eyebrows rose in surprise. 'Well then, it just goes to show you can't always tell a man from his appearance, don't it. And I surely am obliged to you for the warning, Major.'

And then, quite suddenly it seemed, the proceedings came to a close. The Russian soldiers accompanied their leaders down to the shoreline, where boats waited to take them out to the *Politkofsky* and then back to their mother country. They were joined by many of the Russian residents who did not enjoy the prospect of American rule, and so were taking advantage of free transport home. General Rousseau likewise decided that since he had done what he came to do, he might as well return to warmer climes post haste. Perhaps his decision had also been influenced by sight of the available accommodation, because in truth the governor's mansion would have compared poorly to any of those found in San Francisco.

What now remained was harsh reality, as the new administration under Colonel Davis discovered that they really were on the 'Last Frontier'.

CHAPTER TWO

Jefferson C. Davis settled himself proprietorially behind his new desk. With Rousseau on his way back to California, the colonel was the ranking officer with full powers to act as he saw fit. The governor's mansion somehow seemed a very appropriate location for an individual of his elevated status, especially as he was the first American to occupy it.

'Now that all the ceremonial stuff is behind us,' he crisply remarked to Major Thomas, 'we need to stamp our authority on this place. This entire department, or rather country, belongs to the United States. It's like a God-damn empire... with me in charge. And I aim to shake things up around here.'

It occurred to the major that his superior ought to be more concerned with stamping some authority on the enlisted men, who had evidently recovered from the effects of seasickness. Already there had been reports of drunkenness, and violence towards the local inhabitants. The other officers seemed to take a distressingly relaxed view of the behaviour, and he alone couldn't be everywhere.

'It is my intention to make an immediate start,' Davis continued. 'I am informed that there is insufficient accommodation for our men, which is plainly ridiculous and easily addressed. As you probably know, a count has been made, and there are one hundred and sixteen log cabins in this city. Therefore you will requisition all those structures currently occupied by Russians.'

The major regarded Davis warily. He had a bad feeling about this. 'And if they object?'

The colonel's eyebrows rose in surprise at the notion of such irrelevant considerations. Yet beneath his bluff façade, there did lurk a measure of human compassion. He recognized that, with the likelihood of a severe winter approaching, he couldn't just consign a proportion of the population into vagrancy. Conveniently, a novel solution abruptly came to him. 'There's some kind of church at the back of this hill. Am I right?'

Thomas nodded but remained silent. He could see where this was going and didn't like it one little bit.

'So the damned Russkies can go live in there until they get the hell out of Sitka for good. Which they'll have to do sooner or later, because it's not theirs any more and they're not wanted here. Put your men to work, Major, and get it done.'

*

The blue-coated soldiers descended on selected areas of Sitka like locusts. Only this time it wasn't

16

just drunken rowdiness. This time they were under orders.

'There's to be no violence,' Major Thomas reiterated for maybe the third time, before adding the fateful caveat, 'Unless they offer serious resistance.'

The fifty or so infantrymen split up into small squads under the command of a junior officer or non-com. Each enlisted man was armed with a Springfield rifle-musket that had last seen service in the war between the states. Against his better judgement, and recognizing a certain logic, Thomas had agreed that they should fix bayonets. Because the civilians they would encounter spoke little American, it made sense to intimidate them with overwhelming force at the outset and thereby avoid any possibility of uncomprehending resistance.

The soldiers went about their task quite literally with fiery enthusiasm. Darkness having fallen, they spread out on the dirt streets clutching flaming pitch torches. Dispensing with any civilities, they barged into the log cabins, yelling out such simple phrases as, 'Leave now,' or 'Get the hell out of here!' Faced with levelled socket bayonets, the bewildered Russian hunters and traders, oft times with Tlingit native women as their partners, were herded out into the night and on towards the fancily titled Russian Orthodox Cathedral of St Michael's, which was of course the 'church' that Jake had scrutinized at the rear of Colonel Davis's mansion.

Repeated cries of '*Pozhaluysta*' rang out in the cold night air. The soldiers were oblivious of its meaning, and wouldn't have cared anyway. This was one of those all-too-rare occasions when it was actually pleasurable to follow orders, and they intended to enjoy it.

All too aware that his progress under flickering torchlight was likely being scrutinized from Castle Hill, Thomas watched anxiously as the assorted refugees were gradually rounded up like so many steers and driven north along the dirt streets towards the cathedral. Cries of pain erupted, as his men became too enthusiastic with their bayonets and he angrily hollered at them to desist. This business was distasteful enough as it was, without having the blood of innocents on his hands.

Finally their destination loomed out of the darkness, and a non-com eagerly heaved open the double doors. For a few moments, the evicted Russians stared at their new home in bewilderment, not immediately understanding why they were there. Some of their Tlingit consorts displayed real fear. There had been numerous attempts at enforced religious conversion in the past, and they had no idea what these new white masters intended. Perhaps these Yankees followed no religion, and intended destroying the cathedral with them in it.

Not knowing any of their language, the major could only bellow out, 'Go in. Go in. This is your home now.'

Junior officers and then the enlisted men took up his cries, as the extended circle contracted and the cathedral's reluctant residents found themselves stumbling across the threshold. Some of the

Russians must have retained memories or stories of brutal oppression from their homeland, because they too suddenly perceived a much darker purpose behind their enforced presence in the building and began to panic. They picked up chairs and religious icons and began to strike back at the thrusting bayonets.

Quickly recognizing that the mood was turning ugly, Thomas frantically barged his way inside, ordering his men to 'Make way there! Officer coming through,' as he did so.

Arriving within, he was immediately surprised at how spacious the interior appeared. Even with dozens of civilians struggling against their apparent imprisonment, the high dome created an impression of space, emphasized by the light from oil lamps and flickering candles. Shoving a way through the enlisted men, he ordered them to lower their Springfields.

'We mean you no harm,' he shouted at the civilians, desperate to diffuse the situation.

A bearded, bulky individual glared at him. 'Why you bring us here?' he demanded, his words so thickly accented as to be almost unrecognizable.

'Your homes are needed for Americans,' the major replied with genuine embarrassment. 'You must stay here until you… move on.' Even whilst uttering the words, he knew how harsh that sounded. 'Those are my orders,' he added somewhat lamely.

As the wide-eyed Russian sought to make sense of that, those men nearest to him stepped back from the soldiers and demanded a translation. Thomas sighed with relief. With his own men no longer acting so aggressively, the confrontation appeared to be losing its heat. Sadly, though, it was merely the lull before the storm, because whatever the big fellow said to his companions brought forth a storm of protest. A group of them began to rip a pew from its mountings, presumably with the intention of using it against the soldiers.

Abruptly Thomas's patience snapped. He simply couldn't allow this to escalate any further. Reaching for the flap holster at his waist, he produced an army issue Colt revolver. Cocking it, he raised the firearm above his head and squeezed the trigger. The large calibre weapon crashed out in the enclosed space, its unexpected discharge having an immediate effect. As acrid powder smoke mingled with incense, stunned silence descended on the ornate interior.

Instinctively reacting to the shot, the rattled soldiers again levelled their rifles, but their commander was quick to react. 'Hold your fire, God damn it,' he bellowed. 'Stand fast and do *not* shoot!' Taking his lead, officers and non-coms repeated the order. And then, so that no one could be in any doubt, Thomas walked a few steps forward into full view, with his smoking revolver still raised.

The assembled Russians fell back before him, so that for the first time he was able to see deeper into the main body of the cathedral. Even in the poor light, he was abruptly taken aback by the sight of the wall that separated the nave from the sanctuary. Richly adorned with icons and religious paintings, it really was quite magnificent. So much so that for a brief, joyous moment he actually forgot about his real reason for being in the cathedral. But then, as was inevitable, reality intruded on his thoughts.

Recognizing the major's sudden isolation, a young lieutenant and a grizzled sergeant displayed a modicum of initiative by both moving forwards to flank him in support. As the three of them stood there, Thomas caught sight of movement over by the steps leading up to the bell tower. There appeared to be two figures lurking in the shadows. They were most likely clergy, but all his senses were wound up and so he barked out 'Show yourselves!'

The two men slowly turned, and as they did so, light from a kerosene lamp illuminated their features. Their appearance alone was enough to dispel any thoughts that they might be ordained members of the Russian Orthodox Church. That and the weapons in their hands. None of which, though, was enough to explain why Major Thomas's expression abruptly twisted into unmitigated shock, unless perhaps his responsibilities were simply getting to be too much for him. Or maybe it was the fact that these strangers were obviously neither Russian nor Indian. For whatever reason, in a reaction that also seemed strangely out of proportion to any discovery, he again cocked his revolver and howled out a single word:

'You …!'

What happened next took everyone by surprise. Seemingly a volley of gunfire erupted from the far end of the large room, as a rifle and both barrels of a shotgun were simultaneously discharged. Their muzzle flashes flared brilliantly in the poor light. The luckless lieutenant on Thomas's left received a single bullet to the head that blew out the back of his skull, showering those nearby with brain matter and fragments of bone. Stumbling uncontrollably backwards, the young man was dead before he hit the ground.

The major was struck full in his chest by the bulk of both shotgun loads. Its impact felt like a massive, unstoppable hammer blow. Reflexively, his forefinger contracted, causing the Colt Army to discharge a second time. Then, traumatized by the brutal shock, he collapsed to his knees and gazed down uncomprehendingly at the awful destruction inflicted on his body. The front of his army greatcoat had been completely shredded, along with the flesh beneath it. In essence, his torso had been reduced to chopped meat and shattered bone.

Were it not for the fact that the barrels had been shortened by eighteen inches, Thomas would have been the sole recipient of the deadly blast. As it was, the sergeant on his right was also hit by a number of pellets, which tore bloody chunks out of his left arm. As his blood began to flow over the blue chevrons denoting his rank, he let rip a great scream of pain. Neither of the other two victims had emitted a sound.

With blood seeping from the corners of his mouth, Major Edwin Thomas somehow raised his head, as though seeking one last glance at his killer. And then the devastating damage to his upper body overwhelmed him and he toppled forwards to lie still. As pandemonium broke out in the cathedral, the two assassins rapidly slipped around the rear of the bell tower and disappeared into the night. The whole bloody business had taken only a few seconds!

CHAPTER THREE

Colonel Davis hunched forwards in his chair and uneasily regarded the man before him. Steeped in military tradition, he had never particularly enjoyed utilizing undisciplined civilians in support of the army, but sometimes needs must. And this was very much one of those occasions. The newly appointed commander of the Department of Alaska well knew that this was a very bad start indeed for his adminis- tration. Perhaps thankfully, there was not yet a direct telegraph link with San Francisco, Western Union having abandoned the attempt the previous year. So he did at least have an opportunity to catch the assas- sins and determine their motives before reporting the grave incident to his superiors. Which was where this so-called Indian fighter came in.

'As you've no doubt heard, *Mister* Pierce, that bloody fracas last night resulted in one man injured and two dead. One of the latter being Major Thomas, my second-in-command. And we've barely got off the ship, God damn it!'

Jake nodded slowly. He didn't rightly know what *fracas* meant, but he had certainly heard about the gory, and very one-sided set-to in the cathedral. And he genuinely regretted the death of Edwin Thomas. Although not knowing him particularly well, the officer had seemed to be a well meaning and conscientious individual who had taken the time to warn him about the new governor's violent temper. Jake also recognized the distaste with which the colonel viewed him, and yet, not really giving a damn about any repercussions, his response was typically blunt.

'And the fact that you're even talking to me means that you haven't caught the bastards that did it.'

Davis recoiled slightly but, having more pressing matters on his mind, chose to overlook the civilian's disrespectful tone. 'I've had men searching the city all morning. By all accounts there were two assassins, but the problem is that no one really got a good look at them.'

'What about the injured man? Maybe he saw who shot him.'

The colonel grunted. 'Sergeant Beck is in the care of the surgeon. Unless his wounds choose to infect he'll likely survive, but he's heavily dosed with laudanum and witless as a consequence. All I could get from him is that Thomas seemed to recognize one or other of his killers. But how? And, since those men didn't seem to be part of the evicted Russians, why did they react so viciously? None of it makes any sense to me.'

25

Jake thought for a moment. 'It might if they was American.'

Davis registered disbelief. 'What the hell are you saying?'

'I'm *saying* that if the major *did* recognize someone, then they're not likely to be Russian or Tlingit... are they? And what if they've already left Sitka? Have you sent out men to check for any missing boats?'

The soldier blinked in surprise. 'What do you mean by that?'

'We're on an island, right? If they once get off it, they could go anywhere. If they haven't already. Just because your men only saw two of them, don't mean that there ain't more hereabouts.'

The colonel's already harassed features turned ashen. 'Oh Christ!' Anxiety over his own position and possible culpability had clearly affected Davis's judgement, because only then did the magnitude of his task become really clear. 'Sergeant major,' he bellowed out. 'Get in here, now!'

With a half smile, Jake turned to leave.

'Where the hell are you going?' the colonel wailed.

'While you're playing harbour master, I'm gonna see what more I can get out of your injured sergeant.' And with that he strode to the door, stepping smartly aside so as to allow the hurried entry of a man with more chevrons on his sleeves than anyone could shake a stick at.

Davis glared angrily at the departing frontiersman, yet wisely held his tongue. No one of his exalted rank relished being the butt of sarcasm, but unfortunately he had need of Pierce's assistance... for the moment.

*

Having had a number of lead pellets laboriously removed from his left arm, Sergeant Beck was undoubtedly still under the influence of a liberal dose of the opium and alcohol solution that was the most common remedy for acute pain. Yet, under the civilian's astute scrutiny, it was also obvious that the seasoned non-com had been working his previous audience more than a little.

'My name's Jake Pierce, and I'd lay good money this ain't the first time you've taken some lead, sarge,' Jake opined. 'An' I reckon you're in better shape than you'd like folks to think, so how's about giving me a little help, huh?'

The makeshift sickbay had been set up in one of the many cabins confiscated by the army the previous evening. The only apparent luxury that it appeared to possess was a roof. Yet for the patient with his heavily bandaged left arm, residing in it was infinitely more agreeable than having to scour Baranof Island for a pair of elusive murderers along with the rest of his fellow infantrymen. An added benefit was that the sergeant was the only occupant, since none of the newly arrived soldiers had yet had occasion to contract syphilis or any of the other communicable diseases that would doubtless afflict plenty of them before long.

Beck took his own sweet time over a full inspection of his visitor. All he knew of him was that he worked as a scout for the army, and had kept very much to himself throughout the miserable voyage up from California. The non-com reckoned to be a good judge of most men and some females, and what he saw before him was admittedly impressive. This Pierce was easily six feet tall, with a powerful yet lean physique that hinted at both strength and durability. The face was tanned and weather-beaten, and could have been chiselled from granite. His only piece of regulation issue clothing was the black leather belt around his waist with the 'US' legend on its buckle, which in addition to supporting an army flap holster also had a scabbard hanging on its right side containing a massive Bowie knife. And then their eyes met, and the soldier twitched slightly. He sensed intelligence and experience to be sure, but there was something else as well. Beck had witnessed enough violence in his time to know that this man was assuredly a killer, and not just of dumb animals. More relevantly at the present time, he also wasn't some damned officer.

'Okay, okay,' he softly replied, glancing around to ensure that the surgeon wasn't in earshot. 'It's true I ain't in any all-fired hurry to get out of here. Apart from anything else, the laudanum's just too darned good. For the pain, you understand.'

Jake smiled encouragingly. 'What you get up to in here don't matter two bits to me. But what occurred in the cathedral does.'

'You got the job of catching those bastards, huh?'

Jake shrugged. 'Seems likely. It's my kind of work. And most of your men are just simple footsloggers, who've got all on just moving in the same direction together. No offence intended.'

Beck chuckled. 'None taken.'

'So tell me what you recall,' the scout prompted, drawing up a chair and sitting down close to the patient.

The 'buck' sergeant took a deep breath. Even though undoubtedly under the influence of the addictive narcotic, the previous night's events were still very raw. 'The major fired his belt gun into the roof, which put the shits up them Russkies. They backed off, and the lieutenant and me followed him as he moved into the church. Then we saw a couple of fellas near the stairs and Thomas cocked his revolver again. He called out "You!", but before he could say any more, those sons of bitches unloaded on us.'

Jake leaned forwards attentively. 'Did "You" mean he knew them, or was he just gonna add something?'

Beck grunted. 'I get where you're coming from, but I don't rightly know. I *can* tell you a couple o' things, though. Even in poor light, those two hombres looked mean as hell, and I don't reckon they was Russian either, 'cause the lead from that scattergun could have gone anywhere.'

Jake nodded. That supposition kind of fitted in with his own thinking. 'And are you entirely sure you'd never seen them before? Maybe at the ceremony, or around town?'

Beck shook his head emphatically. 'Never clapped eyes on them.' Tentatively moving his arm slightly he added, 'Believe me, I'd know.'

The scout smiled and got to his feet. 'Thanks for your help, sarge.'

That man wasn't quite finished. 'If you ever get them killers under your gun, don't hesitate. You hear? Kill 'em both stone dead for me!'

*

'So did you manage to get any more out of Sergeant Beck?' Davis demanded. He was clearly agitated, which suggested to Jake that there was no good news regarding the whereabouts of the assassins. The civilian decided to give it to the colonel straight.

'Everybody reckons that Major Thomas was the main target because of his rank, and the fact that he said "You!" as though he recognized his killers. But what if he just didn't get the chance to finish? And what if it was really the lieutenant they were after? Think about it. A rifle bullet to the head is a precision kill, whereas a sawn-off is more of a crowd pleaser. It'll make a real mess of anyone it hits, but it ain't always guaranteed to finish them. That said, caught unawares in poor light, if the shavetail *was* the intended victim, then it sure was one hell of a shot!'

The military governor stared at him as though in pain. 'But why would anyone want to murder Second Lieutenant Curtis? It makes no sense.'

Jake shrugged. 'Can't help you there, colonel. But I'll tell you this. If those gun thugs *did* know one or both of your dead officers, then like I said before, it most probably means they were Americans as well. Which gets me to wondering what they were doing in a Russian church. Was it just plain bad luck that they happened to be there when all your men turned up? Really kind of makes you think, don't it?'

Jefferson C. Davis groaned. His head hurt, and despite his instinctive dislike of the rough and ready scout, he had to admit that the man did seem to know his job. Deep in thought, he jumped as a horny hand abruptly rapped on his door.

'There's always someone beating on that God-damn woodwork,' he remarked irritably. 'What is it, Stubbs?'

The sergeant major had news to impart... or rather the man behind him claimed that he did. 'Thought it best to disturb you, colonel, sir. Fella here says he's just seen the cockchafers what did the killings.'

The individual who then shambled uninvited into the big room was like nothing they had ever seen before, and that included the much-travelled scout. Built like and closely resembling a grizzly, on account of the huge bearskin coat that he wore, he had long black hair, which appeared to be liberally greased with animal fat, and features that were almost concealed by a great unkempt beard. Yet there was nothing hidden about the worn Spencer carbine that he clutched with both hands.

Amazed that the supposedly experienced non-com had granted immediate access to an armed man after what had just happened, Jake stepped to one side, his right hand edging towards the flap holster at his waist.

'Hell, mister,' the newcomer boomed. 'You don't need no gun against me. The name's Payne. Cleetus Payne. An' since you're all new to this part of God's creation, I've come to help you. Stumbling in the dark as you are. To prove my *bona fides,* everything I tell you in this fancy mansion is for free, but anything I do for you after that will cost you … plenty! How's that sound?'

The colonel's tired features registered a mixture of annoyance and curiosity. After favouring Stubbs with a severe glance he replied, 'I don't know how you got in here, *Mister* Payne, but we're all busy men. Speak your piece. And it had better be informative.'

If the big man registered the dismissive slur, he didn't show it. Instead he dropped a bombshell. 'The two men you're looking for just left the island. I saw them sneak on to a heavily laden single-masted sailing cutter and head out of the bay. I reckon they'll be bearing southeast to sell their cargo to the Tlingit, or whoever else has got the wherewithal to buy it.'

The federal employees stared at him in stunned surprise. 'That suggests that you know them,' Davis snapped.

Payne guffawed loudly, so that his entire frame appeared to shake. Black chewing tobacco clung precariously to his teeth as he replied. 'I know them for *what* they are, not who.'

'Which is?' Jake queried mildly.

'Smugglers of liquor and guns to barter with the Indians. The Russkies banned the sale of both, years ago, after they nearly got their asses properly whipped by the Tlingit. Right on this very spot where you're sitting, colonel. Quite a set-to, by all accounts. Of course us Americans didn't give two shits about all that. We're just out for profit.'

Davis's eyes narrowed. 'So what does that make you, *Mister* Payne?'

'A hunter of critters, *colonel*. Seals, sea otters, beaver, muskrat, mink... In fact any critters with pelts worth cash money. But right now I've got my eye on government script.' He suddenly turned to scrutinize Jake. 'You look like you've also kilt a thing or two in your time, but unless you know this country like the back of your hand you'll need me... if'en you really want to catch those fugitives. And that's gonna cost.'

Jake returned the scrutiny for a moment before turning to the officer. 'You right set on chasing down those pus weasels?'

Davis nodded vigorously. 'Of course I am. We've only just arrived here, and we need to demonstrate who's in charge. Justice needs to be served, and my officers need to be avenged.' He lowered his voice slightly. 'And my superiors will need to see that firm action has been taken... when they eventually hear of all this.'

The scout grunted, before commenting somewhat acerbically, 'That's what I figured. So I'll get my possibles together while you agree terms with this… gentleman.' To Payne he ruefully added, 'I guess this means another God-damned boat trip, huh?'

That man rearranged his tobacco chaw before grinning broadly. 'It's the only way I know of to get off an island. Unless you Yankees have brought one of them fancy hot-air balloons with you that you used in the war.'

As Jake strode out of the room, Davis called after him. 'Take care, Mister Pierce. The men you're pursuing have proven themselves to be very dangerous.'

'So am I,' came the sharp retort.

*

As Jake Pierce, encumbered by rations and the lethal tools of his trade, reluctantly clambered aboard the small boat, optimistically named *Good Fortune*, all the unpleasant memories of his one and only voyage flooded back and his heart sank. He was an army scout, for Christ's sake, not a sailor!

Cleetus Payne wryly observed his passenger's tortured expression. 'What ails you, my friend? We haven't even set sail yet!'

Jake grimaced, and not just at the prospect of renewed seasickness. He was always wary of overfamiliar strangers. 'Just some bad feelings coming back. Me an' the sea don't get on too well.'

The big man guffawed. 'Puked all the way from Frisco, huh? Well, this trip won't be anything like that. We'll be taking the inside passage through the islands. No open water to worry about, only tides. An' I can handle them.'

Jake glanced around the vessel. What he saw gave him little comfort. For one thing, its far smaller size and draft meant that he found himself much closer to the water than he had been on the *Ossipee*. The *Good Fortune* possessed a single mast and only half a dozen crew, which to his leery eyes didn't seem anywhere near enough. 'There ain't a right lot of men on this thing,' he muttered.

Cleetus spat a long stream of tobacco juice over the side. 'That could be because there ain't many big guns on board, so we don't have to fight the ship,' he responded sarcastically. 'In fact, that Rolling Block Remington long gun of yourn is likely the biggest smoke wagon we got. Oh, an' don't try going below,' he added slyly. 'This deck's all there is.'

A couple of his men exchanged glances and sniggered, but then jumped to it as their boss yelled out, 'Cast off, you sons of bitches. We got another boat to rein in, an' bounty to collect! An' this fella's my guest, so only I get to insult him. An' only in fun,' he quickly added as Jake scowled at him.

With a man on the stern tiller, and the sails set, the cutter surged away from Sitka under the influence of a stiff wind. Jake attempted to ignore the all too familiar creaking sounds of rope and timber under load by putting a question to Cleetus. 'You reckon we've got any chance of catching them?'

With his lank hair blowing in the wind, and spray on his face, the hunter-cum-trader appeared to be in his element. 'Nobody kicked up a fuss when they left, so they've no reason to figure they're being chased. It gives us an edge. That an' the fact that they'll likely be loaded down with whatever they're toting, an' slower through the water.' He glanced up at the scudding clouds and then cocked his head slightly to one side. 'Of course, if we *do* catch them I'll be looking to you an' that *single shot* Remington. Which gets me to wondering why a fella in your line of work doesn't favour a repeater?'

'I don't recall telling you my line of work,' Jake retorted, as he patted his flap holster. 'But I've got one right here. It'll answer fine if anyone tries to rush me close up. The Henry and the new Winchester are fine long guns, but they can be a mite underpowered out in the wild. This Remington never jams an' never breaks, and it fires a fifty-calibre bullet with seventy grains of black powder behind it. That's enough to bring down a buffalo at long range.'

Cleetus nodded reflectively. 'An' I'll bet you can use it, too.'

Jake was about to respond, but instead glanced around him and frowned. 'Why are we headed north?'

Cleetus's hairy features creased into a smile. 'Sharp one, ain't you? 'Cause north is the quickest way to reach sheltered water, that's why. Around the top of Baranof Island, and then south to either British Columbia or on to the good old US of A. That said, I guess *this* is American territory now, ain't it? Hee, hee.' His expression abruptly sobered. 'If I was you I'd get some shuteye. We ain't likely to catch them bull turds 'til late afternoon, an' happen it'll get lively when we do.'

Jake must have appeared dubious, because the hunter quickly added, 'Don't fret, mister. We ain't about to throw you over the side. I'm getting too well paid by your colonel.' And with that Cleetus Payne roared with laughter, before moving off across the deck.

CHAPTER FOUR

A single, none-too-gentle kick to his right foot was all it took. Jake Pierce jerked awake and stared up at the hairy vision looming over him.

'They're up ahead a-ways,' Cleetus Payne announced gleefully. 'I ain't gonna say I told you so… but I did, didn't I?'

Jake shook his head in disbelief, and not just because they had apparently caught up with the wanted men. The fact that he had actually dozed off at sea amazed him even more. But then, peering around, he saw the reason why. Land was clearly visible on either flank, and the cutter's progress through the water was considerably smoother than anything he had so far experienced.

Producing an old, battered spyglass, Cleetus remarked, 'So let's take a proper look-see.'

Clambering unsteadily to his feet, Jake stared down the length of the *Good Fortune*'s deck and out across the expanse of the 'Inside Passage'. Sure enough, far off in the distance, he could just make out the stern of a similar craft to their own. Eagerly he awaited his turn with the glass. Yet when Cleetus finally turned to offer it, triumph had changed to trepidation.

'Jesus! I hadn't counted on that,' he muttered, averting his face from the crew, so as not to alarm them. 'Bastards have mounted a swivel gun. We get too close, they could blast seven shades of shit out of us!'

Jake grabbed the spyglass and strode single-mindedly over to the bow, where he suddenly had to grab for the gunwale as the boat's motion belatedly reminded him that he was still afloat. Sure enough, as he finally focused on the 'enemy' vessel, he caught sight of the diminutive cannon. Mounted on a short stand, it allowed its user to rotate the muzzle across an extremely wide arc, covering any possible avenue of attack. Basically a very large single-barrelled shotgun, it would undoubtedly be lethal against anyone attempting to board... so long as it could be reloaded. And it was that vital consideration that gave Jake an idea. One that became all the more crucial as he realized that their pursuit had been discovered. The smugglers, if that was indeed what they were, gesticulated at each other as they kept looking back.

'Seems like we're gonna turn pirate, don't it, mister?' one of the crew joyfully remarked to him, blissfully ignorant of the deadly ordnance that awaited them.

'That it do,' Jake retorted, deliberately displaying a broad grin as he made his way back to a very pensive Cleetus Payne.

'This ain't gonna work,' the big man softly opined. 'I can't expect my men to go up against a swivel gun. It ain't seemly.'

Jake thrust the spyglass back at him and got up close enough to smell his rancid breath. 'It is if you don't tell them,' he hissed. 'Whoever's on that other boat has spotted us, so we have to get them before the sun goes down. Agreed?'

'Well yeah, but…'

'An' I reckon you're getting very well paid for this, ain't you?'

Cleetus's response to that was rather more guarded. 'Maybe. But…'

'*But* nothing,' Jake pressed. 'All we've got to take is one discharge of that gun. Then I stop them reloading it and we close in.'

'Just like that?' Cleetus retorted mockingly.

'Just like that!'

*

The light was starting to drain out of the sky by the time the two boats were close enough for any meaningful shots to be exchanged. And it was at about that time that Cleetus's crew finally noticed the black swivel gun on the starboard side of the stern, well clear of the tiller. The fact that it appeared to be some kind of relic from the war of 1812 didn't make it any less menacing.

'You bastard, Cleetus!' one of his men roared. 'You never said nothing about us getting our heads blown off.'

'That's because it ain't gonna happen,' that man replied. 'I've got a plan.'

'He's got a plan,' another crewman sarcastically remarked. 'Well, ain't that just a doozy?'

Before anyone could say any more, Jake stepped before them flourishing his rifle. 'Me an' this old buffalo gun'll guarantee your scalps,' he announced theatrically. 'Do exactly as Cleetus says, an' it'll all work out just peachy. You have my oath on it.' He paused to let that sink in before drawing and cocking the Remington single-action revolver from his holster. 'Or we can have it out now, you and me, because one way or another we ain't turning back!'

The crewmen regarded him sullenly for a while, their eyes flitting between the handgun and his set features, as they tried to gauge whether this soldier, or whatever the hell he was, was bluffing or not. Eventually Cleetus decided that they'd figured out he wasn't, because he also went on to the offensive. 'Right, enough fooling around. Let's do this thing. I'll take over the tiller. We're gonna sail right at them varmints, like we're going to board. Only we're not… just yet, anyhu.'

And to start with that was pretty much what happened. With Cleetus at the stern, controlling their approach, and the *Good Fortune* remaining under full sail, they swept on towards their heavily laden prey. Except that, with the latter possessing a swivel gun, the roles might quite easily be reversed.

On the other boat, well aware that they couldn't outrun their mysterious pursuer, the similarly sized crew prepared for a violent defence. Crouched behind the gaping black muzzle with a glowing slow match in his hand, one of them bellowed out, 'Stand off, you sons of bitches, or I'll blow you all to hell!'

Cleetus Payne, with one hand on the tiller and his spyglass in the other, stared intently at the gunner. They were closing fast now. He could sense the eyes of his men upon him, willing him to get it right, for all their sakes. One thing did work in his favour. The swivel gun's advanced age meant that ignition was not by percussion cap. The slow match had to be placed at the touchhole, which *should* enable him to anticipate the blast. And then, quite abruptly, the moment that he'd been waiting for occurred. The gunner's hand moved forward!

Simultaneously, Cleetus heaved the rudder hard over and hollered out, 'Hit the deck!'

Jake possessed the common sense to be already on it, his rifle in his left hand. As the crew dropped down, their vessel swung sharply to starboard, presenting much of its now raised port side to the enemy. Their gun discharged with a tremendous roar, sending bits of jagged metal thwacking into the *Good Fortune's* woodwork, but mercifully missing flesh and bone. Then, as an impressive cloud of smoke blew off on the wind, the scout made his move.

'Bring this thing level and steady,' he barked, getting on to one knee behind the port gunwale.

Cleetus eased off on the tiller, so that his battered craft settled back in the water. Due to the rapid course alterations, the two vessels were now almost parallel with each other. As the gunner frantically swivelled his piece around to reload, Jake cocked his rifle and took hurried aim. Both he and his target were moving, but at such range he was able to compensate. Over on the other boat, a gun crashed out. The projectile chipped splinters out of the gunwale next to him, but he kept his cool. Gently squeezing the trigger, his shoulder absorbed the recoil as he watched with satisfaction the gunner toppling backwards, blood spurting from his chest. Then, with barely a second to spare, he dropped down under cover just as another chunk of lead smashed into the woodwork in front of him. Even while cocking the Remington's hammer and retracting the 'rolling block' to replace the spent cartridge, he instinctively realized that the shooter was likely to be Lieutenant Curtis's killer. And from the rate of fire, the rifle had to be a Henry, or maybe even one of the newfangled Winchesters that he had discussed with Cleetus.

'Put another man on the rudder and get the hell over here with that Spencer,' he barked at Cleetus. 'And keep your head down.'

The fur trader bitterly resented being continually ordered about on his own boat, but he also had other things on his mind. It was dawning on him that maybe he had undercharged Colonel Davis by quite a chunk, because he certainly hadn't bargained on his boat being shot to pieces. Yelling at a member of his now very reluctant crew to take over the tiller, he then awkwardly scrabbled across the deck to join the irritating scout.

'I've got to stop anyone else reloading that swivel gun, but there's another shooter over there and he knows his business,' Jake explained, as he again cocked his rifle. 'And you're too close to me. Move down the side a-ways. We need to stay spread out, savvy?'

Oh, Cleetus savvied all right, but before he could either move or offer an acid response there was another massive crash from across the water and yet more lead spattered the *Good Fortune.* 'Sweet Jesus!' he snarled angrily. 'Who the hell's over there, Wild Bill Hickok?'

Jake risked a rapid glance over the gunwale. He just couldn't believe that they had managed to fire the swivel gun again. His instinct proved correct, because this time smoke drifted away from the gaping muzzles of a sawn-off shotgun. So that clinched it. They were definitely up against Thomas's killers. The question was, could he and Cleetus get the better of them? With a plainly unwilling crew, the only advantage they possessed was greater speed.

As Cleetus crawled towards the bow, Jake fired another shot for effect, all the while desperately thinking of a way to acquire an edge. Any kind of edge. Then it came to him. 'You got any firewater on this boat?' he yelled out, deliberately using the ubiquitous Indian term for whiskey.

Despite their parlous situation, the big man comprehended the inference only too well. Twisting around, he scowled suspiciously. 'What the hell kind of question is that?' he demanded.

Jake chuckled. 'Just funning with you, is all. I want to set that boat afire. A jug of whiskey with a burning rag in the neck of it would likely answer. If you were to have some,' he added mildly.

With understanding came a change of demeanour. 'Toby,' the trader bellowed at one of his men. 'Fetch our passenger a jar of that trade rot gut and an old rag.' A pause. 'And keep your poxy head down!'

As had been the case since leaving Sitka, the *Good Fortune* was still cutting through the water faster than their opponents' craft, and as a consequence had nearly passed it. Which explained why the shooting had tailed off a bit. As an earthenware jug was shoved over to him, Jake again reloaded his rifle and then placed it to one side. 'Can you swing this boat around the front of those pus weasels?' he demanded. 'So I can toss this in as we go alongside.'

Cleetus understood and approved immediately. Such action had another benefit as well. The combined speed, as each craft travelled in opposite directions, would quickly get them well clear of the intended inferno and any return fire. 'Damn right we can. Did you hear that, Clyde?' he enquired of his man on the tiller.

'Oh yeah,' came the reply. Despite the danger, there was no mistaking that individual's growing enthusiasm. This Pierce cuss was not only up for a scrap but he fought dirty, and there could well be a dividend in it for all those aboard... if anything survived the intended conflagration.

Jake discarded the stopper, and replaced it with part of the oily rag. Then he retrieved the precious Lucifers from an inside pocket.

'You'd better not get careless with that,' Cleetus snarled. 'It took me an age to buy this boat.'

Jake completely ignored him. Timing was all, and he would only have a very small window of opportunity. Even as the *Good Fortune* swung sharply to port, the Lucifer burst into life and he applied the naked flame to the rag.

'Get as close as you can,' he yelled at the helmsman. With the turn completed, the two vessels were suddenly rushing towards each other at a tremendous rate. Any misjudgement with the tiller could easily result in a catastrophic collision. Shots rang out, but Jake was aware of only one thing, because the moment had arrived. 'Cover me, Cleetus!'

That man swung his Spencer over the gunwale and loosed off a shot. Before he had time to lever in another cartridge, the scout was on his feet and hurling the firebomb across the narrow stretch of water. Bizarrely, he found himself momentarily staring directly at some gun thug with a sawn-off shotgun. That man was simply too startled by what was coming his way to squeeze the twin triggers. Instead he tried to howl out a belated warning.

The earthenware jug crashed on to the deck and shattered into myriad pieces, its contents instantly ignited by the burning rag. Whatever had gone into the cheap whiskey was extremely volatile, because flames leapt hungrily across the timbers and on to various collections of furs. Yet they seemed to account for only a minor part of the cargo because, in the centre of the deck, a large tarpaulin covered a great deal of something. The individual with the sawn-off screamed in horror as the hems of his trousers caught fire. Dropping the big gun, he turned away in search of something, anything with which to smother the blaze on his person.

Extremely conscious of his own vulnerability, Jake flung himself down just as a rifle cracked out near the opposing vessel's mast. Payne triggered his Spencer again, to no apparent effect, and by then the two boats were fast departing in opposite directions. The big difference now was that one was aflame and the other wasn't. And at sea, in a wooden craft full of combustible material, fire was every sailor's worst nightmare. With the water being so cold, their only possible chance of survival was to make it to land, and luckily for them it wasn't far away. The closest shoreline was on their port side, which was immediately where they made for. And for the pursuing boat there was also no time to waste.

'Turn sharp to starboard,' Cleetus bellowed at the temporary helmsman, but Clyde merely sat with his back to the stern, a strange glassy expression on his face. Then the big man spotted blood on the fur coat, and his heart sank. 'Shit, shit, shit!' he intoned, before scrambling over to confirm the inevitable.

Clyde's particular task meant that, apart from Jake's fleeting appearance, he had been the only member of *Good Fortune*'s crew to remain visible, and he had paid the ultimate price for that. The cutter had only continued on course due to Clyde's dead weight conveniently holding the tiller in place. With surprising tenderness, Cleetus eased the body to the deck. Then, with a look of fierce determination on his grizzled features, he turned the bow towards land.

Jake sensed what was in his mind, and rapidly decided that he couldn't allow it. 'I know you want them dead real bad, Cleetus, but if we pile on in there after them it'll like as not be us doing the dying.'

Only just controlling his simmering rage, that man glared at him. 'So what do *you* propose, soldier boy?'

Jake had that all figured out. 'We follow them in until they get to the shore, and then make certain their boat burns until it's finished for certain. Pick off anyone we can. But once they go to ground, it's us that'll become vulnerable. Under cover, on solid land, they'd be able to blast us all to hell. So we head down the coast a-ways. Go ashore out of range, and get after them on foot.' He paused for effect. 'An' I ain't no soldier boy, mister!'

Up ahead, the other boat was swiftly being engulfed by fire, but parts of it were still habitable. The crew had all congregated at the rear, because to reach land they had to be able to continue steering, and it made sense to stay in one place as they fought the terrifying blaze. One of them had discovered a bucket, and was desperately scooping up seawater with which to douse the inferno. Others frantically beat at the darting tongues of flame with salvaged furs.

Without waiting for a response from the still seething fur trader, Jake took aim with his long gun.

Success was unlikely, given the swaying movement of both craft, but he had to try. Drawing in a deep breath, he held it and squeezed the trigger. The rifle discharged with an encouraging crash, and the wind immediately whipped away the resulting powder smoke allowing him to witness the fall of shot, but the effort initially appeared to be of no avail.

Cursing vividly, he reloaded. Then events took an even darker turn, as whatever lay beneath the tarpaulin ignited with a great 'whumpf', sending tongues of flame everywhere. Seemingly his shot hadn't been in vain after all. Next, the sound of fresh screaming reached them. The blaze appeared to have enveloped one of the fugitives, because he raced for the gunwale trailing smoke and leapt clean over. Immersion in the cold liquid doubtless brought blessed relief from searing agony, but Jake was about to ensure that the man's survival was short-lived. As the *Good Fortune* bore down on the struggling swimmer, the Remington's muzzle poked over the side and this time the result was never in doubt. A large calibre bullet struck the helpless victim squarely between his shoulder blades and he slipped beneath the waves without a sound.

Cleetus expressively spat out yet another stream of his seemingly inexhaustible supply of tobacco juice. 'I reckon that son of a bitch deserved all he got.'

But there wouldn't be any more easy kills like that, because the blazing cutter was about to make landfall. Desperate to escape the unstoppable inferno, the remaining occupants made no pretence at any display of seamanship. Instead they grounded the craft at full speed. Luckily for them, the shoreline consisted of a gentle rocky slope, so the bow merely rode up on to it, rather than smacking into it. Toting their weapons, and as much food and water as they could lay hands on, the five survivors leapt over the sides into shallow water. Jake expended another cartridge in their direction, but with precision shooting impossible, the negative result was entirely predictable.

'That boat will surely burn down to the waterline, an' they'll be drawing a fine bead on us pretty damn soon,' Jake remarked pointedly. 'You need to take us out of here… pronto!'

Cleetus glanced up at him and nodded. His hot temper had cooled, to be replaced by a rather more rational assessment. 'I'm thinking you've done this kind of thing before, ain't you?'

'Plenty. Only this is the first time on water, an' I ain't over anxious to repeat it.'

The big man chuckled as he shoved the tiller hard to port, and not a moment too soon. As the cutter surged away parallel to the coastline, shots rang out on land. Hot lead went somewhere, to be sure, but thankfully none of it struck them. The pursuit was soon to transfer to the mainland, and when it did, Jake Pierce would be back in his natural element. Except that this would be like nothing he had ever experienced before, because, what with nightfall coming on and all the excitement of the chase, it hadn't really occurred to him that beyond the shoreline the terrain was quite literally covered in trees!

CHAPTER FIVE

'So where the hell are we?' Jake hissed. Being in unknown territory under such fraught circumstances didn't sit well with him. Darkness had fallen, and a yellow glow was visible in the night sky to the north. Even though they had to be at least a couple of miles from the grounded cutter and its stranded crew, he instinctively kept his voice low.

'We're on the mainland, for sure,' Cleetus replied in equally hushed tones. 'As to whether we're still in Alaska, well... that's something else again. What with all the islands an' all, the border can get a bit hazy. One thing though, if we're in British Columbia, then the US Army ain't got any say.'

Jake grunted. That was less than encouraging, but wouldn't affect what he had to do. 'An' is there any law hereabouts, if'en we was in that chunk of the God-damn British Empire?'

'Nah. Just this,' Cleetus replied, brandishing his Spencer. 'The John Bulls ain't got around to anything like that, this far west.' He paused to glance around at his waiting men before putting the only question that really seemed to matter. 'You right set on going after them?'

Jake didn't even have to think about that. 'Hell yes! It's what I came out here for, ain't it? Question is, are you coming along?'

The big man flinched slightly. What had seemed like a mighty fine idea in Sitka was becoming markedly less appealing. 'Well yeah, I guess. It's what I agreed with the colonel. An' those cockchafers sure need to answer for what they did to Clyde.'

Despite the poor light, Jake's eyes appeared to take on a strange glinting quality. 'And what about your men?' he pressed. 'How many of them are going with us?'

Cleetus turned to them with a certain amount of trepidation, which turned out to be justified. It was Toby who had the words. 'Like as not, this fella will get you kilt, Cleetus, and I ain't gonna be there when it happens. An' I'll warrant none of these others will, either.'

Although clearly uncomfortable, his companions silently but firmly nodded their heads.

'So that's how it's to be, is it?' the big man snarled. 'An' after all I've done for you, you miserable bastards.' With that he angrily paced up and down for a few moments before recollecting that he really couldn't afford to fall out with them entirely. 'Okay, okay. But at least stay here with the boat until we return. There's vittles a plenty, an' even another jug of bug juice to keep your innards warm.'

'An' what if you don't? Return, that is,' Toby pressed. 'We can't wait the year out.'

Jake had listened to enough. He urgently wanted to press on into the interior for a time, if for no other reason than to ensure that Payne didn't have a change of heart about accompanying him. 'We'll be back within six days, tops,' he barked. 'If we're not, then we won't be coming at all, and the boat will be all yours.'

That was altogether too much for Cleetus Payne. 'Have you lost your God-damn mind?' he exclaimed, angrily grabbing Jake's right arm.

Before the trader could utter another word he felt a sharp pain, as the point of a Bowie knife suddenly probed his neck.

'Don't fret so, mister,' the scout remarked with a deceptively soft tone. 'We'll be back in time. You have my oath on it. But don't ever lay a hand on me in anger again, or I'll saw it off.' With that he removed the blade, but didn't immediately sheath it. That it hadn't drawn blood was a testament to his skill.

Cleetus massaged his neck ruefully whilst he considered how best to react. Finally he decided to bide his time until a more opportune moment. After all, this cuss Pierce was clearly not a man to trifle with, and they did have six days… if his crew agreed. 'Well?' he demanded of their spokesman. 'Are you up for it?'

Toby nodded silently as his gaze flitted between his boss and the Bowie knife. Its blade glinted malevolently in the moonlight.

'So say it!' Jake snarled.

The other man jerked as though he had just been slapped. 'Yeah,' he quickly replied.

Apparently satisfied, Jake collected his possibles from the cutter prior to leaving, but he hadn't quite finished with Cleetus's thoroughly intimidated crew. 'Think on this. If you sons of bitches aren't here when we get back, I'll hunt you all down and kill you. Even if it means swimming to Sitka!'

*

It wasn't long before Jake realized something was amiss. As far as he could discern in the poor light, the land ahead was entirely covered in a great dark mass of trees. Oh sure, there was ample space to move between the huge trunks, but there was no open ground such as he was accustomed to in the great expanse of America's West that he had inhabited. For a frontiersman used to being able to see for miles in any direction it was mighty unsettling. 'Christ!' he exclaimed. 'Ain't there any open spaces around here?'

Cleetus chuckled. He gained a certain satisfaction from the other's disquiet. 'Only if you fell a few trees.'

'And how far do they stretch?'

'All the way to the Coast Mountains. Come sun up, you'll likely see the peaks in the distance.'

'Shit!' That wasn't what Jake had wanted to hear at all. He had thought to move inland a few miles, and then come daylight had hoped to catch sight of the fugitives. 'This sure ain't gonna make life easy.'

*

The two men had walked steadily for an hour or so in a north-easterly direction, which Jake figured would put them somewhere inland of their prey... unless of course those murderous individuals had already anticipated such a move and also shifted position. He knew full well that he was figuratively shooting in the dark, because he didn't know the land or its inhabitants. He was also well aware that he would need Payne's full co-operation if they were to succeed, but the fur trader appeared to be in no mood for conversation. The reality of what he had agreed to was obviously starting to bite. And yet, some things had to be said.

They had arrived at what appeared to be an extensive rocky outcrop. It made sense to camp beyond it, amongst yet more of the ubiquitous timber, so that the rare piece of open ground lay between them and the coast. After laboriously traversing the unyielding terrain, Jake gratefully came to a halt and turned to his companion.

'We've gone far enough for today, I reckon. We'll camp over yonder in those trees. No fire and no noise.'

Cleetus grunted unintelligibly, and after reaching the designated site petulantly tossed his possibles bag into the undergrowth. The unnecessary noise rankled with Jake. 'Just what is it that ails you?' he hissed.

The other man remained silent for a few moments, before finally coming out with it: 'What if they don't come inland at all? What if they head south and make a try for the *Good Fortune*?'

So that was it! The big man's apprehension was understandable, albeit misplaced. 'They ain't got second sight,' the scout quietly replied. 'They can't know where we came ashore, or even if we did. So they're not gonna wander all over God's creation hunting for something that might not even be there.' He gazed at his companion searchingly. 'Don't you think? Huh?'

Cleetus pondered on that for a spell, before slowly nodding his great shaggy head. 'Well yeah, I guess maybe you've got the right of it. I ain't used to this kind of work, is all.'

Jake inclined his head by way of acknowledgement. 'Fair enough. And now that's out of the way, let's eat.'

They both had enough food in the shape of hard-tack and pemmican to stave off hunger. The delights of hot coffee and beans would have to wait for another day. In truth, the prospect of a cold camp held little appeal for Jake, but at least he, like Cleetus, possessed a bearskin coat with which to ward off the October chill. And at such high latitude, winter would doubtless come early. Back in 'Frisco' he had been gleefully informed that further north, in the vastness of mainland Alaska, it got cold enough all year round for his Bowie knife to freeze in its sheath.

Wrapped in their furs, the two men sat just inside the tree-line munching biscuits washed down with canteen water. Almost entirely concealed, and with nothing to give away their position, Jake decided against splitting the night hours into watches. They would likely go short enough of shuteye over the next few days. And so, their brief repast finished, the two manhunters lay down clutching their weapons, and quickly drifted off to sleep.

*

As was his habit when out in the wild, Jake Pierce lay perfectly still when he awoke. Keeping his eyes closed and his breathing steady, so as not to alert anyone who might be watching, he listened intently for anything whatever that didn't sound right. As it happened, noise wasn't an issue, but the smell of wood smoke sure as hell was!

For a brief moment, as his eyes snapped open, he expected to find his large and hungry partner foolishly frying chunks of bacon over an open fire – but that wasn't the case at all. Cleetus Payne lay close by, peacefully sleeping. Then the chill that rapidly came over him had nothing to do with temperature and everything to do with fear. After carefully drawing his revolver, Jake crawled across and placed a horny hand over Cleetus's bristly mouth. That individual struggled briefly, his eyes abruptly wide and bulging in their sockets, until comprehension stilled him. Releasing him, the army scout took his first proper look at their surroundings.

Had it not been for the prospect of lurking danger, the unaccustomed scenery would have been undeniably stunning, with a backdrop of snow-capped peaks just visible through the trees under a clear blue sky.

And yet the only thing that really drew his attention was the single wisp of smoke rising lazily a short distance away to the north. Whoever was producing it was obviously oblivious to their presence, which would hopefully give them an edge when they went looking… as they surely must!

Cleetus had followed his gaze, and was apparently having similar thoughts. Placing his lips close to Jake's left ear he whispered, 'It could be those pus weasels from the boat.'

Jake shook his head, and then replied in a similarly hushed fashion. 'Nah. They wouldn't risk a fire. They'll have to reckon on us being after them. Which means this is something else. An' think on this. If it comes to any killing, we can't risk shooting, for the same reason.' So saying, he angled to one side, holstered the Remington and replaced it with his wicked-looking Bowie. Recalling the previous evening, Payne momentarily stroked his neck before getting to his feet.

A few paces apart, they cautiously advanced through the cedars. As they got closer to the campfire they could discern snatches of conversation, in a tongue that was unintelligible to the army scout. Dropping to their hands and knees they were soon near enough to observe without being seen. It was apparent that this camp occupied a similar position to there own. The wide expanse of rock appeared to be a circular formation with a stand of trees at its centre.

There were four of them around the fire, all decked out in furs and quite obviously some variety of Indian.

One was preparing a form of fried bread known as bannock, whilst the others looked on hungrily. Of more relevance was the string of eight un-laden pack mules that grazed close by near the tree-line. As far as Jake could make out after scanning their surroundings, the animals would remain that way until they received a lot of something to carry. Which meant these God-damned savages were very probably waiting for a certain group of whiskey peddlers to make contact and lead them back to what should have been a heavily laden cutter. And since there was no sign of anything with which to barter, that meant they were all likely to be heading off somewhere together afterwards.

Jake glanced at his partner. Cleetus pointed at the natives and made a drinking motion whilst rolling his eyes. Oh yeah, he too had made the connection. The question was, what should they do about it? For the scout, the answer was obvious, with the desire for a fatal outcome fuelled by his long nurtured bitter hatred for Indians of any tribe. Since the cargo of 'who hit John' no longer existed, along with the boat that transported it, the smugglers would most likely seek to join them, if only to share their provisions and increase the numbers in case of attack. So there really could be only one course of action.

Jake gestured towards the four men and graphically slid a forefinger across his throat. Cleetus's eyes widened in horror. Violence was nothing new to him, and he had accepted it on the water as necessary and unavoidable, but this was something different entirely. They could quite easily just back off and leave the Tlingit to their own devices. Yet Jake Pierce seemed to be unaccountably consumed by some sort of bloodlust.

Although realizing that he was probably wasting his time, Cleetus emphatically shook his head and motioned for them to retire – but the other was having none of it. His eyes gleaming malevolently, Jake clamped the knife blade between his teeth and rose up for a racing start.

'Oh shit!' the trader muttered.

Knowing that the mules' heightened senses wouldn't allow him to get any closer by stealth, Jake took a deep breath and, using both hands, launched himself from the ground and into a dead run. He'd already calculated the killing order, and had complete surprise on his side. Charging into view, with the knife now in his right hand, he kicked the 'cook' hard in his back, sending the luckless Indian sprawling face first into the fire. Ash and sparks showered everywhere. Before the other three could react, Jake leaned to his right and executed a great scything backhand slash. The honed blade sliced through his second victim's jugular, unleashing a veritable geyser of blood. Death for him was almost instantaneous, but such blessed relief would escape the man in the fire. Frantically rolling sideways, he pawed at his ruined face, all the while screaming in agony.

The other two Indians, born to a hard life in an unforgiving land, reacted rapidly to the deadly assault. Both leapt to their feet, grabbing for the nearest weapons. In the case of the pockmarked opponent now facing him, that was a well-worn Colt Army revolver. As the hammer came back with an ominous double click, Jake hurled the Bowie at his torso with tremendous force. The massive blade penetrated this third victim's chest to such a depth that its guard pressed hard against the Indian's buckskin jacket. Emitting a tremendous shudder, he dropped the Colt and seized the protruding handle with both hands, as though fully intending to pull it out.

Jake only dimly registered this, because he was already turning to face the remaining Tlingit warrior. That individual had drawn a wicked-looking skinning knife from his belt. Although very aware that the lone white man had single-handedly dispatched all his comrades, he dropped into a crouch and menacingly advanced. He could see the flap holster on his attacker's belt, and, not realizing Jake's need for silence, knew that he had to prevent any movement towards it. Sadly, what he didn't see was the huge figure looming behind him.

The first the Indian knew of Cleetus Payne's presence was when that man's blade penetrated his back. As the sorely injured native arched upwards in pain, Jake surged forwards, grabbed his wrist and sent the doomed individual's own knife point plunging up through his jaw and on into his brain. Death claimed him instantly, which meant that the last of them had been accounted for.

Yet even then it was far from over. With his third victim now on his knees and still helplessly impaled by the Bowie, Jake's fevered attention was taken by the wailing 'cook'. With his normally bronzed features hideously disfigured, he was effectively blind and almost out of his mind with torment. All that remained to him was to take his own life. To that end, he had dragged an old Colt Navy from his belt with the intention of placing its muzzle to the side of his skull. Still desperate to avoid a gunshot, the scout bounded towards him just as he cocked the revolver.

As the suicidally distraught Indian's forefinger tightened on the trigger, Jake took the only action available to him, and rammed the little finger of his left hand between the hammer and the percussion cap. As the former was released, he endured a stab of pain before wrenching the weapon out of the Tlingit's grasp. Still engulfed by agony, that ruined individual rocked sideways and, with a truly terrible piece of bad luck, fell back into the remnants of the cooking fire. Accompanied by the sickly sweet smell of burning flesh, his screams reached a new crescendo until Cleetus Payne finally silenced them by brutally smashing a rock over his head.

After this brief outburst of frenzied violence, a strange silence settled over the camp, broken only by munching sounds as the hobbled mules resumed their peaceful grazing. Finding it hard to come to terms with what had just taken place, Cleetus gazed around in stunned disbelief.

'Jesus Christ,' he eventually managed. 'I've seen some things in my time, but nothing to rival that.'

Jake, his hands drenched with blood, didn't immediately respond. Instead, his nose twitching, he seized the smouldering Indian by the ankles and dragged him out of the fire. 'This bastard sure got what was coming to him,' he finally remarked with obvious satisfaction, as he wiped his hands moderately clean on the man's leggings.

Cleetus shook his head. 'You got an awful lot of hate in you, mister,' he muttered reproachfully.

Jake looked up in apparent surprise. 'Only for the likes of them. The rest of this is just a job of work.'

The trader decided there was obviously a lot more to that, but this clearly wasn't the time to seek an explanation, if one would even be forthcoming. 'So we've got four dead Indians,' he stated. 'What's next?'

The scout stood up and went over to retrieve his Bowie from the now deceased warrior's chest. 'They don't call this beauty "a sure defence" for nothing,' he opined with evident satisfaction as he heaved on the long knife. With a distinctly unpleasant sucking sound the blade finally came clear. That, too, was wiped clean on the clothes of its victim. Only then did he answer the question. 'When those damn whiskey peddlers turn up, they'll be expecting to see some customers. So we'd better make sure they do. Just who were these fellas, anyhu?'

Cleetus inwardly groaned as he surveyed the blood-soaked cadavers. He couldn't help but feel that events were moving far too fast for him. It was perhaps partly due to the fact that although Pierce possessed no local knowledge he still seemed to be very much in charge.

'My guess is they're Inland Tlingit, but they'll have kin amongst those on the islands, which would make it easier for any gun and whiskey runners to do business with them. Are you fixing on bringing them back to life?' he asked with only thinly veiled sarcasm.

Jake favoured him with a sidelong glance. 'Well yeah. In a manner of speaking *we* are.'

And that was pretty much what they did. The terribly burned 'cook' was dumped in amongst the trees, because Jake intended to take his place. The other three were dragged into sitting positions by using rocks and hacked off branches to support their lifeless frames. Earth was sprinkled over the bloodstains in a mostly successful attempt at concealment. Fresh makings were collected to restore the fire, and then Jake took his place beside it. In his hand was the frying pan, now empty of any bannocks, but at a distance their absence was unlikely to be noticed. His rifle lay ready by his side, because noise wouldn't be an issue in any further encounter.

Cleetus, grudgingly accepting the logic of all this, moved off and took up a position on the western edge of the trees, facing towards the coast. From there it was hoped that he would be able to spot any approach by the perpetrators of the Sitka killings. That was the plan, anyhu!

CHAPTER SIX

Clay Rodeen gnawed on his upper lip as he surveyed the tranquil scene ahead. Smoke curled up from the distant campfire, and the desire for hot coffee, or what passed for it out west, grew within him like an ache. Pretty much all they had salvaged from the burnt-out boat had been their weapons and a small gunnysack of ground chicory, which of course was useless without the addition of fresh water. Natural impatience and the longing to satisfy his desire urged him forwards, but he was held in check by an innate suspicion born of years of hard experience.

'What are we pissing about for?' demanded the grizzled individual at his side. 'We've found them damn savages, ain't we? Let's go eat.'

Rodeen regarded him benevolently. 'Hush your mouth, TT,' he softly responded. 'Things ain't always what they seem.'

The other man peered up at him reproachfully. Had any other cuss told Travis Teague to hush up, he would have 'popped a cap' on him without a second thought, but these two disparate characters were long-time partners in villainy. Besides, his sight wasn't what it had been, and so he supposed that there had to be a good reason for Rodeen's hesitation.

That individual reached into a pocket for his highly prized field glasses. He had obtained them from an army officer in Sacramento some years earlier in lieu of a sizeable gambling debt, and had never had cause to regret his decision. As the Indian encampment leapt a deal closer, Rodeen carefully scrutinized its occupants, and immediately decided that something was amiss.

Although there were four men apparently lounging around the fire, only the one with the frying pan displayed any signs of life, and the high collar of his coat effectively concealed his features. The others might as well have been corpses, and the longer he stared, the more he decided that that was quite probably what they were. Cursing vividly, he transferred his gaze around the treeline. Any number of men could be hidden in there, watching and waiting for his party to draw closer.

Lowering the glasses, he glanced over at his four surviving cronies. To a man they were all watching him, even Grady who was still in great pain from the damage to his legs. Grunting, he came to a conclusion, and as usual with him it would involve his Winchester. After all, someone needed to suffer for the loss of their valuable whiskey cargo.

Since the unforeseen and, as it had turned out, highly unsatisfactory encounter in the cathedral, nothing had gone right for Rodeen and Teague.

They'd only ventured into the so-called 'House of God' to see if there was anything worth stealing before leaving town. Following the departure of the Russian forces it had seemed like a good idea, because the US Army was unlikely to be overly concerned about any theft from a Russian Orthodox church. But then they had seen *him*, and everything had gone for a shit.

Whoever had been sent in pursuit had destroyed their cutter and everything in it. They had two dead and one badly burned, which was why they had remained on the coast until daybreak. What irked him even more was that he knew the owner of the craft that had taken part in the chase. For that matter, the big hairy bastard could well have been on board at the time. And now, to add insult to injury, it appeared that whoever was hunting them thought to spring a trap. Well, that at least wasn't going to happen.

'Take cover,' he commanded. 'It's time to see just who's over there.' And with that, Rodeen tucked the butt of the 'yellow boy' into his shoulder and levered a cartridge into the breach.

Hidden within the treeline, Cleetus Payne had seen everything through his spyglass. At the sight of the raised Winchester he bellowed out, 'Hit the dirt. They're on to you!'

Deliberately tossing the frying pan into the fire to create a diversion of sparks and ash, Jake did just that. Yet the first bullet to come his way hadn't been intended to kill, but rather to provoke a reaction. And since it had been aimed at the fire, it gave the pan a tremendous clout before whipping off into the trees. Jake instantly responded with his rifle, but of course his target had already ducked down.

'Well, that settles it,' Rodeen snarled on hearing the return fire. 'That was some kind of buffalo gun, an' none of them whiskey-sodden savages tote such.' So saying, he levered in another cartridge and snapped off a shot. This time, answering fire came from the trees, and from the speed of it, it had to be from a repeater.

'A little help would be good,' he added, somewhat over-optimistically.

Travis Teague, heavyset and shortsighted, was squatting nearby. He hefted his twelve-gauge before him. 'Be a pure waste of cartridges with this. Besides, I can't even see them sons of bitches.'

The man called Grady, with exquisitely painful, seeping burns to his legs, understandably showed no inclination to get involved. Likewise his two companions, who just shrugged fatalistically. They owned only belt guns, which were little better than a sawn-off when it came to gunplay at any kind of distance.

Although angry and frustrated, Rodeen had to accept the reality of the situation. With all the original occupants of the camp apparently dead, and up against an unknown number of hidden shooters, they were not in a position to win the one-sided gunfight. And there were other considerations as well.

'Grady needs doctoring,' he acknowledged. 'An' we all need vittles. Our best bet is to make for Fraser's Trading Post. We'll be safe there for a while. But the thing is, those bastards over yonder have come into a string of mules, which'll make it real hard for us to outpace them.'

'So shoot the critters,' Teague retorted.

The flurry of shots arrived with breathtaking rapidity. Jake kept his head down until he realized they weren't coming anywhere near him, or even at Cleetus Payne for that matter. Two mules went down without a sound, as though pole-axed, whilst a third emitted a pitiful whimper as its hind legs collapsed beneath it.

'They're killing the mules,' Jake bellowed at his companion. 'Give me some covering fire.'

Without even waiting for Cleetus to comply, he then began tearing up handfuls of grass and threw them on the fire. With the flames smothered, thick smoke began to billow out, obscuring the remaining animals. Keeping low, he raced over to them. More shots rang out, some near, some far. The five uninjured mules were desperate to flee, but were prevented by their tethers. Jake was presented with a dilemma. Cut them loose and he might never see them again. Leave them hobbled and they might all die needlessly. Since they would provide useful transport in the event of the six-day deadline expiring, he really didn't have any choice.

Drawing his Bowie, he scrambled around slicing through the tethers. Several times he narrowly missed having his head stoved in by flailing hooves, but finally they were all free. Instinctively, they noisily galloped off across the rock, away from the shooting and towards the vast forest. Knowing that it was pointless pursuing them until they had settled down, Jake ducked into the stand of trees and made his way towards his 'guide'. Due to the army scout's woeful lack of local knowledge, that was a role that Cleetus Payne would continue to fill for the foreseeable future.

With the two men concealed in the undergrowth, and the mules gone, there was nothing left for Rodeen to shoot at, and so the violent encounter ended as quickly as it had begun. Yet before they departed, the smuggler had a particular itch that needed scratching.

'Is that you over there, Cleetus Payne?' he hollered. 'It was sure enough your boat, you stinking cockchafer!' After allowing plenty of time for a reply that never came, Rodeen expressively spat a stream of phlegm into the dead ground between them. Then the five men simply disappeared back into the trees, and that was that. One moment they were there, and the next they were gone. Swallowed up by the vast forest.

As Jake stared accusingly at the steadfastly silent trader, he retained the rifle in his left hand and allowed his right to drift towards the Bowie in its sheath. They were close enough for the long blade to present a lethal threat. 'You told the colonel and me that you didn't know them fellas.'

Cleetus hadn't missed the ominous movement, but continued to stare fixedly ahead. 'It was just a tiny little lie, is all. If I'd told Davis I knew the killers, he might not have trusted me with the job.'

As though struck by an epiphany, Jake suddenly saw everything with chilling clarity. 'So it ain't just about the specie you're getting paid, is it? You saw a way to put a competitor out of business... permanently. Which means you're in the same line of work.'

Cleetus coloured slightly as he finally turned to meet the other's gaze. 'Maybe I am, but I ain't ever kilt any US soldiers, an' that's what this is all about, ain't it?'

The federal employee grunted his acknowledgement of that fact, but then something else occurred to him. 'And so I'm guessing you knew them God-damn savages as well.'

Cleetus's expression noticeably hardened. 'Some,' he allowed. 'But only by sight. An' it don't give you any call to be fingering that toad stabber.'

Jake ignored that and continued grimly. 'Which is why you wanted me to back off and leave them be. Well, I'll tell you now, that ain't how I work. I go at things in a straight line. So you'd best just get used to that, or we'll end up having a falling out.' Only then did he allow his hand to drop away from the fighting knife.

Having said his piece, Jake got up and began prowling through the trees, pondering their next move. Despite all the new revelations, he could see nothing at all positive in their situation.

'Well, I've got to admit, that whole business didn't pan out like it should have,' he finally announced. 'An' if those sons of bitches get away from us in territory like this we've lost them for good.' He shook his head with uncharacteristic despondency. 'I ain't never seen the like of all these trees. Give me open country anytime.'

'So we're going back to the boat then?' Cleetus enquired hopefully, although deep down he knew he was wasting his time.

Jake's eyes narrowed angrily. He'd opened up too much, and knew it. 'You just don't listen too good, do you? No, we're not turning tail, God damn it.' Another thought suddenly came to mind. 'In Sitka, you said you knew this country like the back of your hand. So now's the time to prove it. We've got five days left before your boat gets a change of ownership, and we're gonna make the best of them. Savvy?'

Cleetus uttered a deep sigh. Oh, he savvied, all right. 'Okay, okay. So maybe there is something we can try.' He paused for a moment to collect his thoughts. 'It don't necessarily matter that they're out of sight, 'cause I could track them through the forest. But there won't be a need for any of that Davy Crockett shit, on account of I reckon I know where they're headed. If you're short on food *and* on the dodge, then there's not many places to go out here. An' they won't want to start shooting critters to eat, in case it brings us down on them. *And* I reckon one of them was injured. All of which means they'll probably head for Fraser's Trading Post.'

Jake knew full well what a trading post was, and what usually counted was *who* was running it. 'So who's this Fraser gonna support? You or the bull turds we're after?'

Cleetus didn't even have to think about that. 'Fraser will favour any side that he decides will benefit him. You working for the US Army won't mean nothing to him... unless you happened to have a chunk of it backing you. Which you don't! Then again, he might smell a profit in Alaska's change of ownership.'

'That's what I figured. Which means it don't really matter who gets there first, so we're gonna try and catch us a mule or three. I've had my fill of this walking shit, and they might could come in handy if we have to move fast with any wounded prisoners.'

'Wounded?'

Jake favoured the other man with a half smile. 'Most of the folks that I pursue don't tend to co-operate until they've been shot.'

*

It was shortly after noon the following day when Hugh Fraser, lean faced and with a shock of red hair, chanced to climb on to the walled roof of his blockhouse. To describe it as a 'roof' wasn't strictly accurate, because there was actually an awning above it, but that was merely to keep the rain off the swivel gun that squatted menacingly on the solid timbers. And unlike Clay Rodeen's now waterlogged piece, this one could boast a percussion mechanism that made it both quicker and more reliable to use.

Fraser had just spent a considerable amount of time and effort arguing over the value of some animal pelts with a couple of awkward Metis who, in his opinion, were too far from their home territory and should have damn well stayed there. Having finally spat on his hand and shaken on a deal, he had left them drinking his cheaply purchased but now vastly over-priced 'rot gut' and gratefully escaped for some fresh air. The reek of grease and faeces that hung over them had at length gotten too much even for him.

Although the business regularly conducted there meant that his establishment was most definitely a trading post, its appearance suggested that it was also a place of refuge. The substantial compound was surrounded by a high stockade, constructed with logs from the trees that had been felled to create the large clearing around it. One corner of it was occupied by the single, large blockhouse upon which he now stood. Smoke curled lazily from the chimney at his side. This building was intended as a defence of last resort in case the rest of the post was overrun, although its strength had never yet been tested. Such a level of fortification was more a testament to Fraser's deep-rooted suspicion of human nature, rather than the dangers likely to be encountered in the Pacific Northwest.

Having peacefully smoked his cherished Meerschaum pipe for a time, he was on the point of returning below when movement on the north-western edge of the forest caught his eye. Five men on foot slowly came into view. One of them appeared to be in a bad way, because a companion on each flank supported him. With the sun behind him, Fraser had little trouble identifying two of the newcomers, which in turn definitely gave him pause.

As the small group drew closer he called out, 'You're looking a little light to me, Rodeen. What happened to the merchandise?'

And therein lay the rub. Not all the whiskey had been destined for the slaughtered Tlingit warriors. A sizeable proportion of it was intended to replenish Hugh Fraser's cellar.

Clay Rodeen ground to a halt and peered speculatively up at the trading post's owner. After a gruelling trek through the forest, constantly on the watch for their pursuers, he had little appetite for bandying words, but recognized that he needed to remain civil... especially under the circumstances. It was only with an effort of will that he managed to restrain himself from glancing back into the trees.

'I'll allow that events could have gone better,' he finally managed. 'We need to lay up for a time, an' Grady here needs some doctoring. So if you'll just let us in.'

Hugh Fraser's spare figure moved not a jot. The stockade's main gate was, of course, barred, and would remain that way until he had reached a decision. Because although the transplanted Scottish Highlander might have lost much of his accent, his shrewd, grasping nature had only been honed to greater perfection during his time in the 'new world', and he didn't miss a trick.

'So who is hunting you?' he suddenly barked. 'Because someone surely is.'

Rodeen's expression didn't alter, but inside he was seething. It angered him that the trader had grasped their predicament so swiftly. It meant that they were effectively supplicants, dependent upon his largesse, which didn't suit at all. Rodeen would happily have shot the trader off his perch, yet that wouldn't do either, for a number of reasons that mostly included money.

'We got into a little trouble in Sitka,' he admitted. 'And that followed us to the mainland.'

'Which means they're still after you,' Fraser stated. 'Otherwise you wouldn't be dragging him around in that condition.'

'Just open the God-damn gate!' Travis Teague snapped. 'I'm so hungry, my belly thinks my throat's slit.'

Fraser lovingly caressed the swivel gun's curves. 'Don't take that tone with me, TT. Or I'll forget that we're all such good friends.' Glancing over at the treeline, he continued, 'How many's out there, and who are they?'

'As to numbers, I can't rightly say,' Rodeen replied. 'But Cleetus Payne might be amongst them.'

Fraser's eyebrows rose expressively. 'Is that what you reckon? Well, it has to be said I find that hard to believe. Cleetus and I have done a little business in the past. He's a canny trader, but I don't see him as some bounty hunter.' He paused for a moment, before coming to a conclusion. 'You got money to pay for your vittles?' Then, as Grady moaned with pain, he quickly added, 'And for one of my men to medicate on your friend?'

Rodeen gritted his teeth. 'We have.'

The makings of an avaricious smile spread across Fraser's lean features. 'Well then, come on in, and welcome.' So saying, he turned and headed for the ladder leading down to the compound. A couple of minutes later, the solid gate creaked open and remained that way just long enough to allow the five men access. Then it slammed shut, and a heavy crossbar was dropped back into place by two of his gun-toting employees, effectively preventing access to whoever else might turn up.

CHAPTER SEVEN

The two men stood just inside the treeline, survey-ing the stockade before them. Nothing that he saw gave Jake any grounds for optimism. Ominously, the imposing log structure appeared to be just as suitable for imprisoning people as keeping them out. And the post's proprietor seemed to take its defence very seriously.

'You folks sure do have a fondness for swivel guns,' he reflected sombrely.

'An' trust me, its owner has got an itch to use it,' Cleetus responded. 'But hopefully it won't come to that.'

That their prey was somewhere inside was not in doubt. Both men had clearly seen the tracks leading out of the forest. Five men, one of them dragging his feet and clearly injured. The fact that they had reached the trading post well ahead of their pursuers had only come about because the latter two men had spent an inordinate amount of time chasing spooked mules across seemingly most of God's creation. They had eventually settled for two of the ornery creatures,

78

and these were now tethered to trees a short ways back. Only time would tell whether they would prove to be worth all the effort.

So the big question was how to proceed. And for Jake Pierce, one thing was glaringly obvious. If anybody was to venture into Fraser's domain it couldn't be Cleetus Payne, because he was known to the smugglers.

As though trying to read his thoughts, Cleetus favoured him with a long, hard look. 'You ain't figuring on us going in there, are you?'

'Not *us.* Just me.'

Cleetus's eyes remained locked on him, but widened dramatically. 'That'd be truly plumb crazy.'

Jake returned his stare. 'Maybe. Maybe not. But I don't see as there's any other way. That cuss with the Winchester...'

'Rodeen. Clay Rodeen.'

'Well, he knows you. So you can't go in. An' we can't wait around out here forever, because we've only got four days before we're left stranded. An' that's if those men of yourn do as they agreed, which I ain't overly confident about.'

Realizing that his companion was in deadly earnest, Cleetus was aghast. 'But what if they recognize you from the boat? I know we was moving real fast, but someone must have gotten a look at you when you threw that jug at them.'

Jake shrugged. 'I'll just have to take that chance, 'cause I don't see any other way. They could be holed up in there for days, an' we can't starve them out.'

'So what story are you gonna give?'

A lopsided smile formed on Jake's features. 'Oh, I reckon I'll think of something. But if it don't pass muster, an' I'm still in there much beyond the slow count of a thousand, you'd better invent a distraction pretty damn fast.'

Cleetus's jaw dropped in almost comical fashion. 'What the hell with?'

Tilting his head towards the blockhouse, Jake remarked, 'I'd bet a month's pay Fraser keeps that swivel gun loaded.' And then he winked before abruptly turning away towards the clearing.

As he watched the army scout walk away, Cleetus shook his head in disbelief. He simply couldn't imagine what motivated a man to take such risks, unless he had some kind of death wish. Then he recalled that he was tasked with assisting him in this mad endeavour, and his heart sank… if only because he didn't know whether he could actually count up to a thousand!

*

Yet another wail of pain reverberated throughout the entire building.

'For Christ's sake, hush your mouth, Grady!' Travis Teague complained angrily through a mouthful of food. 'All that howling is setting my teeth on edge.'

'You're all heart, TT,' Rodeen muttered, but in truth he, too, was rapidly tiring of the excessive noise.

One of Fraser's minions, who professed to a knowledge of healing, was enthusiastically slapping some form of noxious grease on to Grady's exquisitely tender flesh. It was this unfortunate who had briefly come face to face across the water with Jake Pierce. As a direct result of that, the miserable patient now lay along the full length of a trestle table, with the charred remains of his trousers mostly cut away. After the nightmare journey through the forest, all he really desired was the blessed relief of sleep, but that was sure to escape him until the gruelling treatment was completed.

His companions were sprawled about on the rudimentary furniture, shovelling spoonfuls of Sofky into their mouths, and content that someone else was seeing to Grady. They would happily have abandoned him on the trail, except there were some things a man just didn't do once he had sided with another. Because the two foul-smelling Metis hunters hadn't been granted access to the blockhouse, there were no others in the sizeable room.

Clay Rodeen's thoughts were on other things than mere food or even the condition of his employee. He was brooding over the fact that the hospitality of the house had cost him a privately minted California gold piece, taken from a dying man some years earlier. The fact that he had brought about that death was irrelevant. The outrageous charge levied by the poxy Scot simply couldn't be allowed to stand.

A clanging sound reverberated from beyond the stockade's walls, as some newcomer rang the rusty old bell.

'Och, my little trading post is in quite some demand today,' Fraser remarked, a hint of his original origins showing through. Coming out from behind his counter, he hurried out of the blockhouse. His men were under strict orders not to allow entry until he was present, but the fools were entirely stupid enough to forget such things. Stepping out into the compound, he nodded at one of them to issue a challenge.

'Who all's out there?' that man bellowed.

The reply was not at all what any of them might have expected. 'I'm here at the behest of Alaska's new owners,' Jake boldly stated. 'Call it an inspection, if you will. So you'd be mighty wise to open up. And pronto, 'less you want to answer to the US Army.'

Fraser's eyes widened incredulously. This really was turning out to be a day of surprises. Stepping closer to the gate, he remarked, 'I don't know who you are, friend, but you've got my interest and that's no error. Just be aware that you ain't welcome here until I say you are, if you take my meaning.'

Oh, Jake took his meaning all right, and as the gate swung open it came as no surprise to find that he was covered by at least two sawn-off shotguns. With his 'buffalo gun' cradled in his left arm, he slowly moved inside the stockade. 'Start your counting, Cleetus,' he muttered to himself as the gate closed behind him.

There was a lot to take in, as his eyes swiftly scanned the compound and its occupants. The hard-packed earth was broken by a number of huge tree stumps that the trading post's occupiers hadn't had either the ability or inclination to remove. Yet even so, there was room enough within the walls for a corral and a number of lean-tos, as well as the substantial blockhouse.

Four men stood around him. Three of them, scruffy, unshaven cusses, fingered firearms, whilst the fourth stood before him, brazenly looking him up and down. This individual was of medium height, with bushy red hair and lean features. That he was the leader of this gang of cut-throats was immediately apparent, if only because of his eyes. Hard and calculating, they imbued the post's proprietor with recognizable authority. Tucked in the leather belt at his waist was a massive Colt Dragoon, but his hands stayed well clear of it.

'Probably figures he's got me well covered,' Jake decided.

'My name is Hugh Fraser, but you likely already know such,' that man announced. 'There'll be no need for that long gun while you're in my place, so just hand it over to one of my men.'

'One hundred an' three.'

Jake shook his head. 'I reckon not. I keep hold of what's mine. An' you'd do well not to push it, unless you want to tangle with the 9th Infantry.'

Fraser's eyes narrowed slightly as he digested that. 'That's the second time you've threatened me with the US Army. And since you don't appear to have anything to trade, maybe you should tell me just what the hell you're about.'

Jake offered the makings of a smile. 'Oh, that's easy. My name's Jake Pierce. The new governor of Alaska,

Colonel Jefferson Davis, has sent me out from Sitka to take a look-see around his new territory. Being as it's now part of the United States.'

Fraser blinked rapidly as he absorbed all that, and was momentarily lost for words. It wasn't often that he was taken by surprise, but this bit of intelligence had sure done the job. And yet he never allowed himself to remain off balance for long. To give himself a little time, he remarked, 'Jefferson Davis! I'd have thought the Union would have kept him locked up after what he did.'

Jake grunted. 'Same moniker, different fella. Confusing, huh?'

Fraser nodded but didn't comment further on something of little relevance. He had sufficiently recovered from the amazing news to offer a response. 'So the Russkies have finally sold out, have they? Haw, haw, haw. Not that it makes any difference, and I'll tell you for why. I couldn't give two shits who lays claim to this God-damn country. Around here, *my* word holds sway, and that isn't gonna change unless a lot more than just you turns up. All of which means, Mister Government Man, you can eat, drink and be merry, *if* you've got the specie. But then you can be on your way, and I'll just carry on doing what I do as if you never existed.'

Jake smiled conspiratorially before moving slightly closer. 'I hear what you say,' he softly responded. 'And I also know that you're making a show in front of your men. But think on this. With the Russians gone, there's gonna be an awful lot of new money coming up into Sitka. Someone like you could benefit from that, *if* you were to show willing.'

'Two hundred an' ten.'

Fraser viewed the hard-faced scout speculatively. Unsurprisingly, it hadn't crossed his mind that Jake's presence might be connected with Rodeen's troubles, because he hadn't yet heard the full story behind them. It was also a fact that greed was beginning to enter the equation. Perhaps there *was* something in what this stranger said, *if* he was genuine. Ownership by the United States, with its thrusting, dynamic populace, was a vastly different prospect to anything that had been forthcoming from the slumbering 'Russian Bear'. Maybe it *was* worth mellowing a little, while he sussed out his visitor a bit more. Then he chuckled. The California gold piece that nestled in his pocket would more than cover the cost of any vittles offered to this Yankee. And so, in an unaccustomed gesture of bonhomie, Fraser extended his right hand, which was quickly accepted.

'I was perhaps a little hasty, my friend. You're right welcome to share my meagre fare, and I would not seek to disarm an esteemed guest.' So saying, he waved his men away and then gestured for Jake to follow him into the blockhouse.

That man glanced up at the large weapon on the roof and murmured, 'Nice gun!' before trailing his host into the building.

'Three hundred an' fourteen.'

As the post's owner returned to his usual position behind the long counter, the new arrival was suddenly

85

on display for all to see. Sounding uncommonly affable, Fraser asked, 'So, my friend, what's your poison?'

Clay Rodeen twisted around and blinked in surprise at the sight of the tall figure. Casual visitors didn't normally get invited into the blockhouse. Then his eyes momentarily rested on Jake's rolling block Remington and his suspicions were immediately aroused. 'Just who in tarnation are you?' he harshly demanded.

His three able-bodied cronies had pretty much sated themselves on Sofky, and so immediately transferred their baleful attention on to the army scout. Grady, although still in great pain, had exhausted himself and now lay moaning quietly on the makeshift treatment table.

Jake halted just inside the threshold. Slowly and deliberately he scanned the interior. It was as large and solid as it had appeared from the outside. Fraser's long counter stretched the length of one wall. Valuable furs were piled up in one corner, whilst another held the chimney that contained the cooking fire and large pot of stew. In the midst of all this were the five men he sought.

'I just asked you a question, mister,' Rodeen barked.

Concealed within the mantle of his left arm, Jake's right thumb began to tighten on the Remington's hammer.

'Four hundred an' thirty. Four hundred an'... Aw shit! The hell with this.'

Surprisingly, it was Hugh Fraser who spoke next, and *not* to the newest arrival. 'So tell me, Clay, is it true that the Yankees have taken over Alaska?'

Rodeen, with all his attention on Jake, registered disbelief, followed immediately by anger. 'This ain't the time, Fraser.'

That, of course, was completely the wrong attitude to take with the trading post's owner. Suddenly his huge Colt was cocked and trained across the counter. 'Well I say it is,' he rasped. 'Answer the God-damn question.'

Rodeen and his men were abruptly at a loss over the strange turn of events. It was Travis Teague who finally decided to humour their host. 'There ain't no call to get wrathy, Hugh,' he replied in a soothing tone. 'The US of A only took over a few days ago. A large army detail came up from San Francisco in a steam warship, but it was all mighty sociable. There were big guns just blasting off powder, flags waving, an' all kinds of fancy shit going on. You ain't never seen so much gold braid. It was a sight to behold.'

Fraser favoured Jake with a fleeting smile of acknowledgement, before replying, 'Oh aye. And so why didn't you think to tell me all this when you fetched up here?'

Rodeen had had his fill of such irrelevant questions. With his hard eyes remaining on Jake, he snapped, 'There's plenty we ain't told you yet, on account of we was sharp-set.'

'Like what?'

Rodeen sighed with obvious frustration. 'Like how our boat was attacked an' set on fire. Pretty much destroyed, along with everything in it. Like how some cuss with a buffalo gun took agin us on the way here. For all we know it could be him.'

Jake shook his head in apparent incredulity, before glancing over at Fraser. 'Is this how an envoy of the United States is to be treated in your post?'

The proprietor slowly shook his head. 'No. No it isn't.' Although he had done business with Rodeen and Teague for some years, other considerations were coming in to play. Times they were a-changing, and maybe for the better. 'This man is my guest, so you'd do well to keep a civil tongue in your head.'

It was at that moment that fate chose to take a hand. As though jabbed in his vitals by a knife, Grady abruptly jerked upright and stared directly at Jake. His eyes were red-rimmed and feverish, but they were still able to focus on the man who had caused him so much pain.

'It's him!' he screamed. 'The bastard on the boat.'

*

Cleetus Payne couldn't believe that he was actually involved in such a foolhardy ploy. At the side of the blockhouse, balanced atop a very unhappy mule, he had seized hold of the top of the log wall and was attempting to heave his bulk up on to the roof. This wasn't helped any by both the weight of his bearskin and the Spencer slung over his back with a rawhide cord.

Since ceasing the count he had lost track of time, and of course had no idea what was transpiring within. All he did know was that for some strange reason he couldn't just abandon the Indian-hating son of a bitch. Perhaps it was the thought of having to explain Jake's absence to Colonel Davis. Or then again, perhaps not.

With a massive effort, he finally managed to get his upper body over the top, and then drag the rest of him after it. Gasping from the exertion, he lay there for a moment until the thudding of hooves registered with him. A quick glance over the top confirmed his expectation. The mule had taken off towards the forest, and so only the one remained for future use. Sighing, Cleetus got on to his knees and glanced around. He saw two things of relevance. A ladder led down to the compound, and smoke continued to curl up from the chimney. Mercifully, he didn't appear to have been spotted, and so an idea began to take shape.

Rapidly, he checked the swivel gun. A copper percussion cap sat snugly on the nipple above the rounded breach, which strongly indicated that the piece was loaded. Pointing it towards the top of the ladder, he pulled back the heavy spring-loaded hammer. Then, smiling grimly, he took off his bearskin and padded over to the chimney. Then he froze. It suddenly struck him that this really was the moment of no return. He could quite easily just drop down off the roof, disappear into the forest and go back to the coast, where hopefully his boat would be waiting.

After all, this wasn't his fight. The deaths of those two officers meant nothing to him, and no amount of money was worth dying for. But what if, by some miracle, Jake Pierce should survive? Did he really want to spend the rest of his days looking over his shoulder? Then again, was the scout's continued existence likely in such a den of vipers?

'Aw, the hell with it,' he growled, and turned away. Coat in hand and keeping low, Cleetus made his way over to the edge, and then got astride the low wall ready to lower himself back down. Then just as the big man swung a leg over, a flurry of gunshots, mingled with a scream, erupted from beneath the roof timbers.

CHAPTER EIGHT

For a moment all was confusion. Fraser, not really sure what was happening, could only stand by, his massive revolver menacing but strangely impotent. Not so Travis Teague, who was sitting on a stool in the midst of his cronies. He was always ready for a scrap, and this time could actually see his target. Grabbing his deadly sawn-off, he retracted both hammers with practised speed.

At that moment, Jake correctly identified TT as being the most dangerous man in the room, and so reacted accordingly. Cocking his powerful rifle, he swivelled sharply to the right and squeezed its trigger. The Remington discharged with a deafening crash, blasting a bloody hole into Teague's chest and then on out of his back. As the bullet's momentum threw the mortally wounded man backwards off his stool, his forefinger contracted on the twin triggers, indiscriminately unleashing a lethal hail of scrap metal. Most of it struck the log walls and its caulking, but enough tore into one of his companions, putting him on the dirt floor and effectively out of the fight. Clouds of acrid smoke hung in the air as that individual's screams filled the room.

With no time to reload, Jake hurled his long gun at Rodeen, who was even then attempting to draw a bead on him, and then dashed for Grady's trestle table. Barging the startled 'sawbones' out of the way, he grabbed the edge of it and heaved. As the top fell sideways, Grady toppled helplessly to the ground, and a fresh wave of pain overwhelmed him. Squatting down behind the makeshift barricade, Jake drew his revolver.

Fraser, with his big Dragoon already cocked and levelled, had been ideally placed to shoot the scout stone dead, but he was uncharacteristically frozen with indecision. Then something altogether unexpected occurred. Dense smoke began billowing out of the chimney. The trader, always alert to any threat to his livelihood, cottoned on to the reason for that immediately.

Ignoring the mayhem within, he raced for the door and bellowed out to his employees, 'There's someone on the roof. Get up there, you morons!'

Then as he turned back into the increasingly smoke-fogged room, it suddenly came to mind that maybe there was a connection between whoever was up there and this Jake Pierce. Which had to be a sound enough reason for him to at least put a ball into one of his extremities and slow him up some.

Cleetus Payne had heard Fraser's shouted command, and so was ready for anything that came up the ladder. Balanced in his left hand was the cocked Spencer, whilst his right gripped the swivel gun's lanyard. Over the chimney mouth lay his heavy bearskin. It hadn't occurred to him when placing it there that Jake Pierce was just as vulnerable to suffocation as anyone else. And if asked why he was still present, he probably couldn't have answered, but it was enough that he was. Footsteps sounded on the rungs of the ladder. It was nearly time.

The head and shoulders of his first victim appeared above the low wall. As he saw the gaping muzzle, that man's cautious expression turned to one of absolute horror. All he could think of was to drop back down, but a companion was close behind and in any case it was already too late. Cleetus yanked on the cord, and the gun emitted a mighty roar as it strained against its iron mounting. With the full load *and* muzzle flash striking him at point-blank range, Fraser's luckless employee was literally torn to shreds.

As the blood-soaked corpse fell back out of sight, Cleetus clambered forwards and pointed his carbine over the side. He caught a brief glimpse of a shocked figure staring up at him, and quickly squeezed the trigger. The bullet struck that fellow just above the bridge of his nose, flattened it out some and then blew out the back of his skull in a welter of bone fragments and gore.

Some raw instinct of self-preservation told Cleetus to back off, and it was that reaction that saved his life, as a twelve-gauge crashed out somewhere in the compound. He actually heard the charge pass over his head before he hunkered down to lever in a fresh cartridge from the Spencer's magazine. There had to be at least one more opponent down below, in addition to whoever was in the blockhouse. But one thing was for sure, they wouldn't be in there for much longer!

It was the sound of his own swivel gun discharging that finally tipped Hugh Fraser over the edge. Whoever the hell was up there had to be connected with this Yankee cockchafer, who apparently possessed an enviable talent for lying, and now appeared to be intent on wrecking his property and killing the rest of his customers. Any thoughts of prospective gain finally fell away, to be replaced with raw anger. That was fuelled by the fact that by now he could barely see, and was choking on the thick smoke that filled the room. Again backing off to the only door, he stood in the threshold, aimed at Pierce's last position and deftly emptied all six chambers of his Colt Dragoon. The gunshots crashed out in rapid succession, releasing yet more smoke and leaving his ears ringing painfully.

Fresh screaming confirmed that he'd hit someone. But then, as he reluctantly retreated out into the fresh air, two figures, both coughing uncontrollably, appeared out of the murk and barged past him. They turned out to be Clay Bodeen and his only remaining able-bodied crony. The fact that they were unable to talk allowed Fraser time to peer around the compound, and what he saw wasn't encouraging.

Two of his employees lay near the foot of the ladder leading up to the roof. Or at least he assumed that was who they were, because the entire upper body of one had been obliterated, and the other fellow, having been shot in the face, was only recognizable by his clothes. A third lurked near one of the lean-tos, nervously clutching his weapon. Although shaking his head with disbelief, Fraser still had the presence of mind to close the heavy door, thereby trapping the smoke inside.

'You poxy madman,' Rodeen finally managed to gasp. 'Firing blind into the smoke like that, you could have killed me.'

'Never mind that,' Fraser retorted dismissively. 'There's some maniac on the roof slaughtering my men. And why is that Yankee soldier trying so hard to kill you?'

'I'll tell you all about it when they're both dead!'

*

Jake Pierce lay flat on the floor, a kerchief over his mouth and nose. He knew that if he remained in the blockhouse he would soon pass out. Yet to leave through the only door was to invite certain death. Then it came to him. A grasping cuss like Fraser was sure to have a cellar for the storing of high value merchandise that shouldn't really be in his possession. If he could locate it, get down into it, and then wait for the smoke to clear, he could maybe catch off guard those who ventured back into the building. It was obvious to him that the entrance to any such hideaway would likely be away from prying eyes, behind the counter... and so it proved.

With his eyes closed but still streaming, he crawled in that direction, initially hitting his head against solid wood, but finally coming around the rear of it. Feeling his way forward, all the while with his lungs seemingly on fire, he suddenly came across a square of timber with an iron ring at one side.

'Thank Christ,' he murmured, getting on his knees and heaving on it. The effort left him light-headed and reeling, but he persevered. As the trapdoor lifted, Jake tugged the kerchief down below his chin, and with blessed relief smelt the smoke-free musty air. Dropping on to his chest, he thrust his head down and drew in a deep breath. Then he rolled over and bellowed up at the roof. 'Enough with the smoke, Cleetus! You hear?'

A moment later, and to his intense relief, he heard the muffled cry of 'Yo!'.

*

Clay Rodeen glared angrily at Fraser. All four survivors stood in the lee of the building, so as not to present a target to the assassin above.

'Did you hear that, you Scottish faggot? We got Cleetus Payne up there. Like I done told you before, him an' that other bastard are working together. Killin' my men an' yourn.'

The recipient of that slur gripped his empty Colt with impotent rage. If it hadn't been so, he would have undoubtedly 'popped a cap' on the insolent whiskey runner. As it was, his inability to do so highlighted the fact that his ammunition supply and spare weapons were all in the blockhouse!

Fraser glanced over at his remaining employee. That man licked dry lips, and apprehensively grasped his sawn-off. The gruesome remains of his two companions lay before him for all to see.

'You got powder and shot for that?' his boss demanded.

'Some.'

'Well then, he shows himself, you blow him off the roof.' Then, raising his voice, Fraser added, 'You hear me, Cleetus? I'm mighty disappointed that you've taken against me. We've never had a cross word afore now. So when we've settled your friend, we'll see to you. Even if it means burning my own building out from under you!' With no reply forthcoming, he turned to Rodeen. 'I'm not forgetting what you said to me, but we need to work together on this. Everybody in there ought to have long been dead by now, so unless that Pierce character has lungs of leather we shouldn't have anything to fear from him. Then again, I'm not the trusting sort.' With that, he kicked open the door and then, as thick smoke drifted out, he recovered one of the discarded shotguns and checked that it was loaded.

With the obstruction obviously removed from the chimney, it wasn't long before the interior became visible again. As expected, there were a number of corpses strewn about, some killed by hot lead and others by suffocation. Both the sawbones and his patient had expired, the former brought low by one of his own employer's randomly discharged balls. Strangely though, none of the cadavers appeared to be the self-proclaimed United States envoy.

*

It was pitch black in the cellar, and mercifully free of smoke, but Jake knew that he couldn't remain down there. Having survived where others hadn't, he now had to be ready for whoever came looking, and thankfully his revolver was fully loaded. With his heart seemingly pounding like an anvil strike, he felt for the wooden ladder. The underground store, although apparently not very large, was quite an elaborate affair, having been partially boarded out with rough-cut timber to prevent the roof collapsing. Purely by touch, he had discovered a number of crates and kegs stashed around the walls. Their contents would undoubtedly be worth further scrutiny, if he lived to get the chance!

With the Remington in his right hand, Jake climbed two steps and then used his skull to ease the trapdoor up slightly. It was immediately apparent that the air was clearing. Cleetus had obviously done as instructed, *and* it appeared that the solitary door was open, which could mean only one thing. An unknown number of assailants were coming to kill him, and so he had better be God damn ready!

*

The three men rushed into the room and fanned out, nervous and trigger happy. Even Clay Rodeen wasn't immune to this apprehension, because despite being no stranger to killing folks, he recognized that they were up against a very dangerous individual. And what with the trestle table tipped over, the various piles of merchandise and the dead bodies, there was no shortage of places for concealment. Hugh Fraser had deliberately positioned himself on the left so that he would be nearest his counter. He had a shrewd idea just how Pierce had survived, and in spite of his own very real fear, he fully intended to be the man who killed him.

As the others carefully scanned the now pretty much smoke-free interior, Fraser crept around the nearest end of the counter and suddenly smiled. The trapdoor was wide open. In such a confined space, his sawn-off would turn anyone down there into chopped meat. Any damage to his stored possessions would just have to be tolerated. Coming up behind the hatch, he thrust the big gun over the opening and...

Jake swung round the far end of the counter, his right hand extended, and fired once, twice. The two shots in rapid succession cut down the trading post's proprietor before he even knew what had happened. With a faint cry, the mortally wounded man fell forward, straight down into his own cellar. His shotgun was conveniently thrown towards his killer, mercifully without discharging.

Jake reached out to grab the big gun, and then twisted round to face the way that he had come. Whoever else was in the room now knew roughly where he was, and so it was unlikely that they would risk coming over the top of the counter, or that they would be fully upright. Therefore it was time to take a real chance. After holstering his revolver, he checked that the percussion caps were properly seated on the nipples of the twelve-gauge, and then moved back to his end of the barrier. Drawing in a steadying breath, he momentarily paused at the sound of an exchange of shots beyond the walls. They confirmed that Cleetus was still in the fight, but the outcome couldn't affect what happened next.

Launching himself forwards, Jake landed flat on the ground between the counter and the fireplace. Right in front of him, roughly six feet away, Clay Rodeen's stealthy figure was approaching. His belt gun was pointed in the correct direction, but the muzzle was too high. And in the time it took for him to lower it, Jake had squeezed both triggers. The massive discharge scythed into Rodeen's lower legs, quite literally blowing them from under him. Traumatic shock flowing from the shattered limbs brought about a contraction of his fingers, amongst other things, and his revolver discharged harmlessly into the ceiling.

As the inevitable screams filled the blockhouse, Jake remained on the 'deck', but discarded the smoking shotgun and drew his Remington single action. The sole remaining antagonist stood a few feet from Rodeen and regarded the prone figure with a mixture of awe and horror. Dropping his weapon as though it were a red-hot coal, he turned for the door and ran. Jake, who neither knew nor cared which faction the nameless fugitive belonged to, viewed his rapid departure with indifference. He hadn't yet adopted the practice of shooting unarmed men in the back. And besides, not knowing who remained outside, it seemed like a good idea to conserve his ammunition.

*

Cleetus Payne heard the initial ruckus below and knew that he couldn't remain on the roof. Yet he was all too aware that a deadly sawn-off shotgun awaited any move that he might make. Feeling strangely light-headed, he desperately searched around for anything that could be utilized. Although used to a hard life in the wild, this level of violence far exceeded anything he had ever encountered before, and there was an unpleasant tightness across his chest. His fevered glance fell on the murderous swivel gun, but even loaded that would have been no use due to its fixed position. Then he saw his discarded bearskin and felt a glimmer of hope. Falling from above, it could just be mistaken for a body, at least for a crucial second or two. It would have to do.

Grabbing the heavy coat, Cleetus deliberately stomped about near the outside ladder for a moment, and then abruptly hurled it out over the edge. Even as he sidestepped to the right, there was a crash as the shotgun discharged, and then he poked the muzzle of his Spencer out over the low wall. As he had so fervently hoped, his opponent stood directly below, pointing the double-barrelled weapon at the ladder. Although he clearly had the drop on him, Cleetus didn't hesitate for an instant. Aiming at the largest target, the man's torso, he squeezed the trigger. And yet instead of a satisfying crash, there was merely a muted pop. Misfire!

It would have been hard to tell just who was the most shocked, but what really counted was who would recover first, and even more relevantly, whether Fraser's man had discharged both barrels or only one. Cleetus didn't wait to find out. Frantically, he levered out the dud cartridge. As a fresh one entered the breach, he cocked the carbine and swung to one side to avoid the empty twelve-gauge that had been hurled up at him.

With the gun thug below now frenziedly reaching for his revolver, Cleetus rapidly drew a bead and squeezed. This time there was no difficulty. As the smoke cleared, he saw that he had struck his victim full in the chest, knocking him back and then down. And yet, even with bloody froth coming from his lips, that individual stubbornly attempted to cock his weapon. Sighing regretfully, Cleetus again went through the motions and lined up for the kill shot. At the prospect of another senseless killing, he was tormented by a very real anguish.

'You stupid bastard!' he yelled. 'It doesn't have to be like this.'

But of course it did, because the terribly injured man displayed a dogged determination to raise his weapon. And so yet again Cleetus's Spencer crashed out, and this time the outcome was inevitable.

For a moment, as he stared down at his now very dead opponent, there was silence. Then more gunshots reverberated in the room below, and he recognized that, like it or not, he would have to leave the roof. After quickly working the under lever with trembling hands, he made for the ladder. If he hadn't been so pre-occupied, Cleetus might have thought to glance around the clearing beyond the stockade. Had he done so he would possibly have noticed furtive movement on the treeline. As it was, he descended two rungs at a time, completely oblivious to the possible menace that lurked in the forest.

The lone, unarmed individual who burst from the blockhouse had wild, terrified eyes, and quite plainly presented no threat. So, just like Jake before him, Payne allowed him to run. And run he did. Out of the stockade, and on across the clearing. The big man grunted, and then moved over to the threshold. The sound of screaming was very audible, and so he bellowed out:

'It's Cleetus Payne. Who all's in there?'

The response wasn't quite what he might have expected, but it did at least bring a relieved smile to his hairy features.

'Well, you took your damn time! You call that a distraction?'

CHAPTER NINE

'You've shot me to pieces, you miserable cockchafer!'

Jake Pierce gazed down implacably on his writhing prisoner. It was his opinion that Rodeen ought to consider himself damn lucky. Due to a lethal combination of hot lead and dense smoke, there were no other survivors out of all the occupants of the trading post. The pair of Metis traders, who earlier had so tested Fraser's patience, had sensibly fled the compound after the first shot.

'Well yeah, it does look to me as though you've taken on board a shit load of metal,' Jake coolly agreed. 'An' whether you make it or not, kind of depends on how you answer my questions.'

Rodeen's bloodshot, pain-filled eyes stared up at him. His legs were peppered with shot and bleeding badly, and the left one appeared to be broken. But due to the size of the individual projectiles, his injuries were survivable... *if* he was to receive treatment. Failing to take any comfort from his assailant's words, the injured man then gazed searchingly around the room.

'So where's that turd, Cleetus, gone?'

Jake shrugged. 'Seemed like he'd had a bellyful of killing, so I sent him out looking for a mule. If I should agree with myself to patch you up, we'll likely use it to tote you back to the coast.'

Despite his visceral hatred of the man before him, Rodeen was struggling to cope with the intense pain. His desperate need for relief really left him with no choice. 'What do you want to know?' he spat out.

'That's the spirit,' Jake remarked lightly. But then his deceptively affable demeanour rapidly changed to one of pure menace. 'Why'd you gun down those two American officers in Sitka? What were they to you?'

Rodeen shook his head, as though such matters were of little account. 'We'd never clapped eyes on them before. They were just unlucky, is all. We were only in the damn church 'cause we thought it was a good place to keep clear of the military till we left town. There wasn't even anything worth stealing. How were we supposed to know the blue bellies would turn up with a load of Russkies?'

The scout stared at him intently. 'Then why?'

'Because they just happened to be there,' the other man shouted. 'It was that poxy sergeant who was supposed to die, an' only then 'cause he chanced to see us!'

'Beck?'

'The very same.' Rodeen glanced over at Travis Teague's body. 'An' we'd have got him too, if TT had shot straight.'

Jake was mightily puzzled, and in more ways than one. 'How could he have missed with a sawn-off twelve-gauge?'

With obvious effort, Rodeen managed to peer up at him scornfully. Sweat was pouring from him, and he was clearly in a bad way. 'Why'd you think TT favoured a scattergun in the first place? 'Cause he couldn't see worth a damn!'

Jake blinked. 'So why Beck?' he persisted.

The wounded man's head dropped back against the dirt floor, and his eyes began to glaze over. Plainly it was not an act. He was at the end of his tether, at least for the present. Emitting a gentle sigh, his head then lolled to one side.

'God damn it all to hell,' Jake exclaimed, before bending over to check Rodeen's pulse. One existed, and he supposed that he'd better keep it that way, at least until he'd obtained an answer to that last question.

*

How much time had passed, he'd no idea. After a great deal of feverish activity, Rodeen's legs were tightly swathed in bandages, fashioned out of clothing stripped from some of the less badly used cadavers. Jake had made no attempt to extract any of the lead shot, or even splint the broken leg, because in truth he didn't care whether the man lived or died. The wounded trader just needed to survive long enough to answer one important question.

The door burst open without warning, causing Jake instinctively to reach for his revolver. Cleetus Payne shambled into the room. He was red-faced and agitated, and from the way his chest was heaving, had clearly been running. Part of his bearskin coat had earlier been shredded by the shotgun pellets fired at it when he was on the roof. Under other circumstances he would have cut a comical figure, but his expression alone was enough to banish any levity.

'What ails you, Cleetus? Looks like you done seen a ghost.'

That man shook his massive head emphatically. 'The dead don't frighten me none. It's the living that give me pause.' He stood for a moment, swaying slightly and getting his breath, before spilling out his story in a rush. 'I went looking for that damn mule, like you said. Thing is, all I found was the fella that ran from here. What was left of him, anyhu. He'd been gutted and scalped. It was a fearful sight to behold. An' there was no animal to be seen. What's worse is, I reckon those that done it are still out there... waiting on us. I could feel them watching me.' He suddenly appeared slightly shamefaced. 'An' that's the which of why I was running.'

It didn't take Jake long to reach an unsettling conclusion. 'Appears to me like it's maybe more of those Tlingit, out to settle scores for what we did to their friends.'

Cleetus nodded unhappily. 'Damn right. An' I'll tell you something else. I don't like all this killing. 'Cause when you kill folks, you end up with their kin coming after you, an' it just goes on and on.'

Jake regarded him askance. 'Is that a fact? Well, happen you should have told this son of a bitch,' he remarked, indicating Rodeen's still unconscious form. 'It's on account of him we're out here in the first place.' And with that he turned and headed for the door.

'Where the hell are you going?' Cleetus snapped irritably.

'I'm gonna see about reloading that swivel gun. We don't know how many savages are out there, so we can't leave now and risk spending the night in the forest. And there aren't enough of us to defend the whole post. So we'll have to sleep on the roof. Keep an eye on that skunk, an' if he wakes up try to find out what he and his friend were up to in Sitka. That's if he'll still talk to you. Ha, ha.' And with that he was gone.

Cleetus glanced uneasily at Clay Rodeen's still form, before perusing the rest of the room. He shivered. It was like a God-damn charnel house. To occupy himself, he began to collect up the various weaponry. With the Tlingit apparently out for blood, he and Pierce would need all the help they could get returning through the forest. In fact, since any fighting would be at close range, a brace of shotguns apiece seemed like the best option.

*

Up on the roof, Jake did the necessary. Powder, shot, an old rag for wadding, and a fresh percussion cap.

Then, with a theatrical flourish, he swung the deadly 'crowd pleaser' around so that its muzzle pointed at the trees. Raising his arms, he bellowed out, 'Come on you heathen bastards. Show yourselves!'

Unsurprisingly, there was no movement on the treeline. What did occur, however, was far more disturbing. From beneath his feet there came a single gun shot. Vengeful Indians forgotten, he quietly padded over to the ladder. After rapidly descending, Jake drew his revolver and approached the door. All was unsettlingly silent.

'Will I torch the place?' he harshly demanded.

'Hell no,' Cleetus retorted. 'What is it with you an' fires, anyhu?'

Jake cautiously entered the blockhouse and discovered a very unhelpful turn of events. The latest in a series of them in fact. Under a fresh cloud of smoke, Clay Rodeen still lay on the dirt floor, only now it wasn't just his legs that showed damage. A fresh hole had been blown in his chest, and this one had proved to be fatal.

'Oh shit!' Jake exclaimed. 'That's just dandy. I thought you'd had your fill of killings.'

Cleetus shrugged apologetically. 'He left me no choice. Woke up and reached for a gun while I had my back turned. If he hadn't been hurting so bad, I reckon he'd have got me for sure.'

'Couldn't you have just winged him?'

'Hell, I ain't *that* good with a firearm. I'm a business man, not a gun hand.'

Jake shook his head in disgust, and began prowling around the big room like a caged lion. 'You know what this means, don't you? I never got to find out why him an' that other fella wanted a sergeant called Beck dead.'

Cleetus registered surprise. 'They did?'

'I just said so, didn't I? An' because of it, two officers died instead. Which begs a mighty big question. What had happened between Beck and Rodeen?' Jake abruptly ceased pacing and turned on Payne. '*You* wouldn't happen to have any idea, would you? After all, you an' him were in the same line of business.' As he let that hang in the air, his eyes narrowed. The cocked revolver was still in his hand.

Although well aware of that, Cleetus nonetheless bristled with anger. 'Just what the hell are you getting at?'

'Dead men can't talk!'

'Would you rather I was dead in his place?'

Jake smiled grimly, but didn't answer, and for a long time the two men just stared at each other. It was the outside world that finally intruded. Through the still open door it was obvious that daylight was on the wane. The scout sighed. No good could come of the stand-off, and there were other considerations. Besides, he'd just had an idea.

'We need to eat and then get up on the roof with some of Fraser's blankets and all the guns we can carry. It's gonna be a cold night, and it *might* be a dangerous one as well. But first we need to get that sack of shit outside.'

'What the hell for?'

'Because if he stays in here he'll start to turn all the faster, an' I want him back in Sitka looking like he could still be alive.'

That was too much for Cleetus Payne. 'You want us to tote a dead man through that forest, with Tlingit looking to lift our scalps?'

'You got a better idea how to find out what Beck's been up to?'

*

The two men passed an unsettled night on the roof, taking it in turns to keep watch. As far as they could discern, no one approached the stockade, but the light from a small fire flickered enticingly in the trees. Jake briefly contemplated replicating his previous attack on the Tlingit camp, but decided against such a risky course of action. It could easily have been a trap, and in any case he had no idea of their numbers.

The long hours of darkness did give him some time for reflection, and he concluded that he might just have been a bit hard on his companion. After all, Cleetus *had* stayed to help him when he could easily have cut and run for the coast. And yet there remained that little niggle in his mind about the circumstances of Rodeen's death.

The new dawn brought no respite from the chill, and so found them momentarily unwilling to cast off their blankets. But then a vision of Rodeen's waxy features came to Jake, and he knew that they needed to

112

be on their way. Although the blockhouse roof was pretty much unassailable, to remain there would mean missing the rendezvous with Cleetus's cutter, which was unthinkable. Apart from any other considerations, there needed to be a reckoning with the mysterious Sergeant Beck, because he was obviously a non-com with some dubious secrets. And to make that work, Jake would need Rodeen's uncomprehending assistance.

As expected, all the cadavers were stiff as boards, and the one of particular interest to them also flaunted its left leg at an entirely unnatural angle. 'We've got about three days before he starts to bloat,' Jake opined. 'If that happens before Beck sees him, then my plan's just so much toast.'

Together, the two men heaved the wholly uncooperative corpse on to the back of one of Fraser's mules, which they had selected from among three others that were stabled in a lean-to at the far side of the compound. Jake had agreed with himself that those animals would be released into the clearing just prior to their departure, in the hope of distracting attention from themselves. It was a sad fact, though, that any such ploy would be of only temporary benefit.

'So how do you think they'll try to take us?' Cleetus put the question as they heated up the remains of the Sofky. Although Jake was keen to depart, he had recognized that it made sense to start what could be a very testing day with a hot meal.

'You're asking me?'

'Yeah, I am. 'Cause you seem to have a knack for killing folks.'

Jake grunted. It was true, he *did* have a singular talent for causing carnage, but it only really ever gave him pleasure when his victims were red skinned. The rest of the time it was just business. 'I reckon those devils will let us get into the forest, an' then rush us from all sides. It's what I'd do. Then agin, savages don't often think like white folks. But however you cut it, a couple of shotguns each ought to put a scare into the murdering varmints.'

Cleetus had begun to spoon hot food into his bowl, but glanced curiously at his companion. It was time to ask a certain question. 'Where's that hatred of Indians come from? From what I've seen, some's good an' some's bad, just like white men.'

'That's what you reckon, huh?' Jake's eyes flashed with sudden anger, and for a moment Cleetus reckoned the other man might attempt to strike him. 'Well, I could maybe see how a man might think that… unless he'd lost all that was dear to him at their hands.'

Cleetus blinked but held his tongue. He sensed that he was about to get an awful lot more than just Sofky for breakfast.

'You ever hear of the Sand Creek Massacre in Colorado?'

Surprised, Cleetus nodded. 'Even this far west, we heard about that. Some bluecoat name of Chivington made a real name for his-self by killing a shit load of Indians. Men, women and children all, as I recall. Him an' his men cut them up something awful.'

Jake favoured him with a chill smile. 'Oh, he did that all right. An' the folks back east said he was a bloodthirsty murderer who should answer for his crimes. Funny thing, though – the further west you got, the more people thought he'd done a mighty fine job. Including me. 'Cause earlier that year, a band of Cheyenne dog soldiers had turned up at a cabin in eastern Colorado an' butchered my wife an' two young uns. An' there ain't a day goes by that I don't think about it. Or the fact that I should have been there to protect them, instead of sashaying around with the army. So now, whenever I pop a cap on some Indian, or slide this big knife into his guts, I just see it as there's one less of the bastards on God's creation.'

Cleetus stared at him wide-eyed. He hadn't expected such a candid disclosure. 'So why'd you suddenly tell me all this? I kind of reckoned you had no liking for me.'

The army scout shrugged. 'Just a whim, is all. We don't know how many of them dirt worshippers are out there. One or both of us could die today, so it seemed right that you knew a bit more about me. 'Cause there sure as hell won't be any markers left in the forest. Besides, you might be a bit of a pain, but we do make a pretty good team.'

CHAPTER TEN

The three animals were strangely reluctant to leave the confines of the stockade. It was as though they sensed an impending change of ownership and didn't approve. Cleetus whacked the hindquarters of the rearmost with the barrel of his Spencer, and finally the mules trotted off across the clearing. Since they were veering to the left of the two men's escape route, Jake kept their own beast, along with its gruesome cargo, on their left flank as a form of shield. He reasoned that since the Tlingit were likely to value the mule either for their own use or in trade, they would not wish to injure it. That was his fervent hope, anyway.

It was also with thoughts of their opponents' potential avarice that they deliberately left the gate wide open, in the hope of encouraging some serious looting and therefore delaying any pursuit. Although as Jake acknowledged, 'If they've got any sense, they'll come to conclusions with us first. Then they can take their sweet time over the rich pickings in there.'

And with that in mind, there was one other task that he had attended to before they left. In a brief survey of the cellar, he had discovered a large array of firearms and whiskey kegs. Certainly enough to be of interest to Sitka's new governor. And so, with Cleetus's help, he had heaved the unresisting Fraser out, closed the trapdoor and placed the body across it. Then, in the hope that superstitious Indians might be wary of tarrying in a building full of corpses, he dumped another blood-soaked cadaver next to it.

Their mule was not just for transporting Rodeen's blanket-shrouded carcass. It also carried two spare shotguns, leaving them with one each, in addition to their own weapons. Since only their personal long guns used the latest metallic cartridges, all the others would be awkward to reload in any kind of running fight. And neither of them was under any illusions about what lay ahead.

Crossing the clearing, they heard the noises associated with rapid movement off to the left in the trees, confirming that the Tlingit were definitely still in the area. The sounds gradually decreased, indicating that Jake's initial idea had worked. The warriors had indeed gone after the precious mules. Not that he felt any optimism as the, to his mind, forbiddingly oppressive forest again engulfed them.

'I sure didn't misremember how bad this was,' he whispered gloomily, as they moved ever deeper into the primeval surroundings.

Of the previous night's fire there was no sign, but a slight smell of woodsmoke lingered menacingly in the air. Jake Pierce had taken part in any number of punitive expeditions against various Plains Indians. It was because of his lethal skill that no less a person than Major General Henry Halleck, Commander of the Military Division of the Pacific, had assigned him to accompany Colonel Davis to Sitka. Yet when making that decision, the general hadn't taken into account the fact that any warfare against the Tlingit or Athabascan tribes of Alaska would be more akin to the fighting back east during the French and Indian War of the previous century. Taking on an unseen enemy in dense forest required a whole different set of skills. Thankfully, Jake had the capacity to adapt, and was accompanied by someone who possessed a sound knowledge of woodcraft.

As the two men and their mule padded swiftly westwards through the seemingly endless trees, Cleetus quietly remarked, 'I ain't doubting your talent for killing, but if… *when* they attack, it won't be about trying to keep our distance. We'll need to go to ground and hit back. Savvy?'

Jake nodded thoughtfully. 'I can do that. I'm just glad you know the lie of the land, 'cause I freely confess I don't.'

Cleetus favoured him with a genuine smile. 'If anything happens to me, just keep heading west, and eventually you'll hit the coast. Whether you'll be anywhere near my crew is another matter.'

'If they've waited for us.'

Cleetus didn't reply, because in truth he wasn't sure himself, but didn't want to admit it. And from then on, with more pressing matters to think on, they remained silent, as both men strained to see or hear anything that might indicate an imminent assault.

For some two hours they continued on through the forest. The almost palpable tension increased with every step covered, until it reached a level where they actually welcomed some form of attack. Although it was fully light, not much of it seemed to penetrate the canopy above. At ground level there was a dispiriting gloom, which Jake hadn't noticed so much on the way out, but which now seemed to emphasize the sense of extreme menace felt by both fugitives. Because that, in effect, was what they now were. The tables had most definitely turned!

From somewhere at the rear a twig snapped, and for a brief moment both men froze. And then, because happenstance simply couldn't be accepted in such a fraught situation, they reacted fast. Jake tethered their mule to the nearest tree, and then dropped to his knees behind another. Cleetus did the same a few feet away to avoid bunching. Both placed their shotguns within their coats to muffle the sounds of the hammers being cocked.

As though mocking their efforts at concealment, an arrow abruptly slammed into the tree a few inches above Jake's head. He dropped lower, but held his fire. 'I can't even see them,' he exclaimed.

Two more shafts flew harmlessly past Cleetus's position. 'Which means they can't really see us,' he retorted. 'They're just trying to spook us into breaking cover.'

119

Both men recognized the Tlingits' tactics. The Indians were deliberately favouring arrows over fire-arms to avoid any telltale smoke, but with no reaction forthcoming they didn't spend long over it. There was a sudden rush of feet as a pair of buckskin-clad savages clutching hand axes raced towards Jake, each taking a flank so that at least one might manage to cleave his skull. Cleetus Payne, similarly under threat, was unable to offer any assistance.

As he had already amply demonstrated, one thing the scout knew about was fighting. He also knew when to move. Leaping to his feet, he rapidly backed off so that the angle between his two assailants was not so wide. Then he levelled the sawn-off, pointed it slightly to his left and unleashed the corresponding charge. The squat weapon belched forth death out of one barrel, throwing the hurtling native off his feet, his torso bloodily peppered with shot. From off to the side, another shotgun crashed out as Cleetus also fought for his life.

Swiftly shifting the big gun in a lateral arc, Jake just had time to register the look of absolute horror on his second victim's swarthy features before he squeezed the other trigger. At such close range, the dark result was brutally predictable. After absorbing the entire shattering blast, the dying man twitched and jerked on the ground for a few moments before laying still.

Jake glanced to his left and saw that Cleetus was engaged in a frantic struggle with a Tlingit warrior who had managed to deflect and then seize hold of his twelve-gauge before he could fire it. Hastening over to them, he viciously slammed the butt of his empty weapon against the Indian's skull and was rewarded by the sound of breaking bone. With his grip on the shotgun no longer disputed, Cleetus triggered his second charge in the direction of a number of fleeing warriors. Since they were moving fast amongst the trees, the scattergun failed to score a fatal blow, but it left them in no doubt that he had the continued ability to strike hard.

And then, as swiftly as they had come, the Tlingit were gone, and peace of a sort returned to the forest. Clouds of acrid smoke gradually dispersed as they rose through the trees. With the fighting ended, Cleetus appeared dazed by such intimate bloody violence. All the feelings of revulsion that he had experienced at the blockhouse returned. Swaying slightly, he breathlessly managed, 'Now what?'

Jake paused for a moment to draw breath, and somehow he instinctively knew what to do next. 'We need to move on fast while they're disorganized. We've given them hard knocks, but I reckon there's plenty more of them out there. There sure ain't time to be reloading these.' So saying, he gripped his empty muzzle-loading shotgun by the business end of the barrel and swung it hard at the nearest tree trunk.

The iron twisted under the force, irreparably shattering the trigger mechanism. Cleetus followed suit with the same result. Both then grabbed their loaded replacements from the back of the mule, before untying it and quickly resuming their march west. And this time there was an even greater urgency to their pace, because now there was no doubt at all that they were being pursued.

Jake knew all about following a trail across open country, and so was mightily impressed by Cleetus's skill in such markedly different terrain. Sometimes they appeared to be travelling through virgin forest, whilst at others there was at least a discernible track of sorts, but he never once hesitated. And all the while, the Tlingit no longer made any attempt to hide their presence. First from one flank and then another came blood-curdling howls that set the white men's teeth on edge. And then the sniping began.

A firearm crashed out from somewhere behind them, and a section of bark flew from a nearby trunk. More shots followed, the hot lead getting closer all the time. Since the old saying that 'Indians couldn't shoot worth a damn' was patently untrue in that part of the world, it surely could only be a matter of time before a projectile struck flesh and bone.

'Sweet Jesus,' Jake exclaimed. 'These devils really are out for blood, ain't they?'

'It must be something you did,' Cleetus responded dryly.

'It sure as hell is something I'm gonna do!' With that, the army scout handed the mule's reins to his companion. 'Pass me that scattergun. I'm gonna teach them sons of bitches not to tangle with the US Army.'

Surprised and puzzled in equal measure, Cleetus accepted charge of the mule and handed over his weapon.

'You might cover me with that Spencer, huh?' Jake added. His own long gun was carried across his back to allow freedom of movement, which he was going to need in spades. After cocking all the four hammers of his shotguns, he hefted one of the heavy guns in each hand, took a deep breath and abruptly raced back the way they had come. Cleetus was quite simply appalled, but knew better than to protest. Instead, he did the only thing he could and tucked the butt of his carbine into his shoulder. Although diligently searching for a target, he was still able to witness the most amazing display of courage that he had seen, or was ever likely to.

Jake had consciously emptied his head of debilitating doubts and fears. He knew that his actions were those of a madman, but didn't see any other way out of their predicament. If the Tlingit were not hit again and hard, they would continue to snap at the fugitives' heels until it was their blood that was spilled. Survival relied on continued progress towards the coast.

That he had caught the Indians by surprise was not in doubt. As the scout ran through the trees he glimpsed a band of fur-clad natives. One of them spotted his approach and then the others turned towards him in stunned surprise. It was unheard of for a lone white man to 'count coup', and yet why else would this one be making straight for a vastly superior number of enemies?

But then all such musings were suddenly irrelevant, because Jake was in amongst them like a berserker.

Holding a heavy sawn-off in each hand meant that taking considered aim was impossible, but with such fearsome weapons it really wasn't necessary. In rapid succession he loosed off one barrel on each flank. In the relative gloom of the forest, the muzzle flashes flared brightly as the deadly loads tore into the mesmerized Tlingit. As two of their number collapsed in bloody agony, the remainder frantically attempted to scatter. But at close range, there just wasn't any escape from a scattergun. Their terrible assailant again levelled his twelve-gauges at the fleeing Indians. Yelling out, 'Run for your lives, you worthless cockchafers!' he squeezed two more triggers.

Yet again the shotguns belched forth death, and two more opponents fell to the ground with multiple wounds. Only this time they were shot in the back, but since they were Indians, that wasn't something that troubled Jake. At that point, with the war party quite literally on the run, he should have immediately high-tailed back to his companion. But he was overcome by an excessive bloodlust that hadn't yet been satisfied.

Advancing on his nearest victim, he dropped both firearms and drew his Bowie knife. Bending down, he entwined the clawed fingers of his left hand in the moaning individual's lank hair and brutally yanked his head back. This was going to be all the better because the man was still alive.

'For Christ's sake get back here,' Cleetus bellowed, but he might as well have addressed the man in the moon.

Emitting a strange cackle, Jake made a rapid series of semi-circular cuts into his victim's scalp. Then, with a triumphant howl, he heaved a bloody section of it clean off. The pitiful wreck beneath him released a great moan and crumpled to the ground, never to rise again. As though leading a charmed life, his killer gleefully waved the hideous trophy at the remaining Indians, who had by now ceased their headlong flight. Only belatedly did he recollect that he was still vastly outnumbered.

'That's enough, Pierce, you crazy bastard,' Cleetus pleaded, and this time he got a result.

Scooping up the empty shotguns, Jake began to retrace his steps. And he nearly made it too. With only a couple of yards to go, he felt a hammer blow on his left arm and cried out in pain. Stumbling badly, he just managed to remain on his feet, but dropped both of the hefty firearms in the process.

With his Spencer, Cleetus Payne drew a bead on the Tlingit who had winged his companion and squeezed the trigger. Through the resulting smoke, he was just able to make out the 'fall of shot'. Dropping the abruptly unmanageable long gun, the Indian fell back clutching his left shoulder, which was close enough to count as an 'eye for an eye'. Rapidly levering in another cartridge, Cleetus fired again and that was enough to send their remaining pursuers back into the trees. How long that would last was, of course, anyone's guess.

Blood soaked the scout's coat sleeve, but this wasn't the time for doctoring. Leading him over to the tethered mule, Cleetus barked, 'We can't wait around to patch you up. Use this critter for support and get walking that a-way.' After releasing the animal, he covered the few paces necessary to recover both shotguns. Then he took the time to scrutinize their back trail.

The only Tlingit still in sight were either dead or dying. After shaking his head in dismay at the continued need for bloodletting, Cleetus finally turned away and followed his staggering companion. He had already decided that come what may, they had to keep moving until nightfall. After the grievous casualties that the Tlingit had suffered, it seemed unlikely that they would attempt to close in on the two white men in the dark, especially if the latter maintained a cold camp. That might well be hard on Jake, because it meant his wound would not be cauterized should it require it – but such was the cost of unnecessarily claiming a scalp.

*

It was only by calling on all his reserves that Jake had been able to keep going, but as darkness began to fall he could walk no further.

'If I don't stop, you'll have another corpse on your hands,' he mumbled. His left arm felt as though it was on fire, whereas his legs possessed all the mobility of lead.

Cleetus nervously scrutinized the seemingly impenetrable forest behind them. There was no sign of their vengeful shadows, and in truth there hadn't been since their last bloody set-to. Yet he had little doubt that they were out there somewhere, because although Indians wouldn't normally accept heavy fatalities, there was something different about this war party. Perhaps their leader had lost a relative amongst those originally waiting for Rodeen's party. Then he glanced at Jake's abnormally pale features, and reluctantly accepted that they had to call it a day. Tethering the mule to a tree, Cleetus helped ease his dog-tired companion to the ground.

'I need to take a looksee at that arm before we lose all the light,' he announced softly.

And so, over the scout's protests, he began to remove that man's coat. The bullet-torn left sleeve was sodden with blood, which doubtless explained his weakness. And as the big man sliced away the material around the wound, he realized that there were both good and bad aspects to it. The lead had gone straight through, leaving an apparently clean hole without any fragments of clothing visible. But it was a sizeable one and there was a possibility that the bone had been clipped. Dousing it with whiskey, followed by exquisitely painful cauterization was the preferred option, but out of the question due to the lack of both fire and fiery liquid.

'This needs a hot iron on it, but we can't risk any flames,' he explained to his light-headed patient. 'So I'm gonna have to bind you up as tight as I can to stop the bleeding, an' hope that it holds 'til we get back to Sitka.' He felt like adding '*if* we get back', but held his tongue.

The clothes on Rodeen's corpse provided the makings for a bandage, and by the time it was truly dark the painful wound was firmly bound. It meant that Jake would be unable to move the arm, but then there was little strength in it anyway.

'You won't be using that rolling block rifle of yourn for a time,' Cleetus opined. 'Best keep that holster gun to hand in case they hit us again tonight.' Even as he said it, he recognized that if such a thing happened they would be in serious trouble. As it was, all he could do was reload the shotguns and settle down to wait for daylight. It was going to be a long, cold night, but if they survived it then the next day should see them back at the coast. Whether his men would be there to greet them was something else entirely!

CHAPTER ELEVEN

'How many days has it been?'

The unexpected question took Cleetus Payne by surprise, because he hadn't realized that Jake was even awake. Dawn had finally broken, and light was beginning to filter down through the trees. The hurting and exhausted scout had slept the whole night through, and Cleetus had let him. He, on the other hand, had passed the hours of darkness on watch, although if pressed he would have admitted to having dozed a little. Consequently, he wasn't at his best, and had to think hard for a moment or two.

'That was our fourth night,' he eventually replied. 'Which makes this our fifth day since leaving the *Good Fortune.*'

'So those sons of bitches have got no excuse for not being there.'

Cleetus bridled slightly at the abrasive tone. The cutter's crew were, after all, his men. So it was acceptable for him to denigrate them, but not someone else. 'How's about you and me get to the coast before we start cussing them, huh?' Turning away, he began a careful scrutiny of the surrounding forest.

On the face of it, all was still. There had been no threatening movements in the night, and as far as he could tell, they were on their own. All of which meant doodly squat when Indians were involved, but didn't alter the fact that they had to get moving again. And due to his injury, it appeared that Jake Pierce was no longer the 'push hard' that he had been.

'Come on, you lazy bastard!' Cleetus rasped. 'On your feet. We can eat when we're walking.' So saying, he took the scout by his right arm, and none too gently hauled him upright.

A piece of lead slammed into the tree trunk next to them, spattering their faces with fragments of bark. The gunshot was accompanied by howls of derision, but it was difficult to tell just how far away their tormentors were. The two white men desperately searched for a target, but none appeared, and after a few moments the forest fell silent again.

'Just letting us know they're still around, I guess,' Jake calmly opined. But nevertheless, when they again resumed their westward journey, his right hand tightly grasped the only weapon that he could usefully handle: his Remington single-action revolver. Although his mouth was crammed full of delicious pemmican, he didn't really savour the taste, because all he could think of, as he doggedly kept pace with his companion, was when the cursed savages would likely hit them again. As though taunting them, he had managed to tie the severed scalp to the tail of the mule. Despite their parlous situation, the sight of it somehow gave him hope. He might never have encountered the Tlingit before, but just like every other heathen dirt worshipper, they could be beaten!

*

They walked all morning and on into the afternoon, until Jake felt sure they must be going the wrong way, clean across Canada to the Atlantic or whatever the hell else was over that way. Then out of the blue, Cleetus suddenly announced, 'I can smell it, God damn it. Salt water.' He paused, stuck his nose in the air and then, as the delightful reality sank in, favoured his companion with a broad grin. 'Huzzah. We've only gone and done it!'

Jake didn't get the chance to comment on that momentous discovery, because it abruptly became brutally obvious that the Tlingit agreed. And they recognized that this was their last chance to finish what the white men had started. A fusillade of shots rang out, and some of the lead struck flesh and blood: the valuable mule pitched forward, shot twice and dead before it hit the ground. With darned bad luck, its bulk landed on the legs of the uncomplaining corpse.

'Leave it and run,' Cleetus commanded. 'Those bastards ain't fooling around any more!'

Jake's response was not at all what he might have expected, and demonstrated that some of the old vim and vinegar had returned. Drawing his revolver, the scout dropped down behind the two bodies, using the mule's bulk as cover. 'I ain't going anywhere without Rodeen,' he angrily retorted. 'This stiff's my only chance of finding out what all this was about.'

The big trader stared at him in disbelief. Numerous figures were moving about in the trees, and more shots rang out. This wasn't the time for heroics. And yet, after all they'd gone through, he couldn't just leave him. 'God damn you, Jake Pierce,' he exclaimed, and not for the first time, but nonetheless moved to join him. 'Cover me!'

So saying, he pushed his hands under the cadaver's armpits and heaved with all his considerable strength. Rigor mortis had long since set in, and actually assisted him, and the body began to work loose from under its crushing burden. And not a moment too soon.

Jake's revolver bucked in his hand, as he fired at the nearest shadowy figure. He hadn't supposed he would hit anyone, and therefore wasn't disappointed when he didn't. His task was to buy them some time. And it worked because, with a triumphant cry, Cleetus suddenly had the rigid body free. The big man realized what had to come next, and he grimaced with revulsion. Seizing the torso, he lifted the now uncovered corpse over his right shoulder. He swayed backwards slightly under the unwieldy burden, and at that moment a bullet struck Rodeen's back with an unpleasant thwack. The dead man had effectively saved Cleetus's life.

'This tarnal cockchafer has finally come in useful,' he muttered, before stepping out for the coast.

Jake, knowing that they now had too many weapons to carry, awkwardly picked up each shotgun in turn and discharged all four barrels at their attackers. Cloaked by clouds of smoke, and with his ears ringing painfully, he then left the scatterguns where they lay and followed his companion. It would be just his bad luck if the Indians possessed the makings to reload them. Over his right shoulder were slung the two long guns, which would have to suffice until they were taken aboard the *Good Fortune*.

Except that, when the shore finally came into view, there was no sign of the vessel. With extraordinary skill, and despite being under frequent attack, Cleetus had led them to the exact spot where they had left the cutter and its crew. And yet, only five days on, those men had apparently reneged on their agreement.

'The poxy sons of bitches,' Cleetus raged. He had deposited his gruesome burden amongst the rocks, and was gazing out over the open and empty water in disbelief. 'If I ever catch up with them, I'll skin them alive.'

'I thought you didn't hold with killing,' Jake retorted as he unslung their weapons.

That they would still need them became unpleasantly clear, as yet more shots rang out. The Tlingit were scattered around the treeline, taking care not to show themselves. And in truth they didn't need to. Although shielded by rock clusters, the two white men literally had nowhere left to go. All their hopes had rested on the *Good Fortune* being present.

Lost in thought, Cleetus remained upright, glaring impotently at the 'Inside Passage'. Far from being their escape route, the expanse of water was now an insurmountable barrier. Hot lead began to ricochet off nearby stones, but still he didn't react.

'For Christ's sake, get down,' Jake yelled. Proffering his Remington 'buffalo rifle', he added, 'See what you can do with this, unless it's too much gun for you.'

Cleetus finally came to his senses and belatedly took cover. Accepting the single-shot firearm, he sighed and retracted the hammer. 'Seems like there's no end to this killing.'

An Indian unwisely appeared from behind a tree with a levelled weapon, and the trader gently squeezed off a shot. The heavy bullet flew unerringly to its target, irreparably puncturing a lung and removing yet another Tlingit from the fight. A collective howl of outrage rang out around the treeline. The fine shooting served as a reminder that they would do well to stay under cover and just keep the white men pinned down.

Cleetus flicked back the breechblock and extracted the smoking cartridge case. As Jake handed him a replacement, the trader grunted. 'I can see why so many fellas like these guns. It's got a good feel to it. Question is, be it enough?'

Unsurprisingly, given his debilitating wound, Jake was unusually slow on the uptake. 'What do you mean by that?'

'We can't eat it or drink it!'

And that actually cut right to the heart of the matter. These warriors really were persisting beyond what was normally expected from warring Indians, but surely sooner or later they would realize that against such determined opponents a siege was the best option. All they had to do was keep the white men bottled up on the shoreline and wait for their food and drinking water to run out.

As the chill reality abruptly hit him, the scout blinked once very slowly. He'd been in some tight corners in his time, but this one would take some beating... if he survived it. With a wan smile he remarked, 'Any suggestions?'

*

The answer to that question came about thirty minutes later, and from a most unexpected source. The two men were hunkered down next to their 'chief witness', apprehensively awaiting the Tlingits next move. Jake's left arm throbbed abominably, and blood seeped through the bandaging. He would have sold his soul for a draft of laudanum, but abruptly had something else to think about as a voice hollered out from some distance behind them.

'Bet you thought we'd gone off an' left you, eh Cleetus?'

The beleaguered pair twisted around, and for a moment both were literally speechless. About one hundred yards away, the *Good Fortune* was slowly approaching the shore.

'Cat got your tongue?' the man whom Jake remembered as Toby yelled out. There were guffaws amongst the others, which suddenly stopped as fresh gunfire broke out in the trees.

Cleetus finally found his voice. 'I'll allow I'd given up on you fellas, but we can jaw on that later. For now, just get the hell over here, pronto!'

And that was exactly what the crew did. But even with the craft close in, it still meant that the shore party had to scramble some way across rocky ground before entering the water. And since one of its members had irreparably lost the power of movement, Cleetus went first while Jake covered him.

'What the hell are you toting that sack of shit for, boss?' came the not unreasonable query, as Rodeen's battered corpse was roughly dumped on to the deck planking.

Cleetus, now cold and wet, was in no mood to bandy words. 'Because Jake Pierce reckons it'll be useful. An' what he wants, he gets. Savvy?'

Entirely bewildered, Toby could only nod.

Jake fired another ball into the forest from his revolver, and then made a break for it. With two long guns again slung over his shoulder, his gait was awkward and slow, but at last he made it into the chill water. After wading unsteadily out to the vessel, he threw his weapons over the gunwale, and then allowed himself to be painfully dragged aboard. There were more shots from the forest, and a projectile lodged itself in the cutter's woodwork.

'Holy shit, those bastards are shooting at us,' the man on the tiller wailed, as he swung the rudder over.

'You don't say,' Cleetus drolly responded as the *Good Fortune* caught the wind and pulled strongly away from the coast. 'They've been shooting at *us* for days! An' just where the hell were you when we needed you, anyhu?'

It was Toby who shrugged and then gestured at Jake. 'Got bored of waiting. We went looking for that boat he burned out, to see if there was anything worth scavenging. Then we heard a noise,' he added, which had to be the understatement of the decade.

Cleetus offered some mild rebuke that the weary scout didn't attempt to comprehend. Instead Jake purposefully shuffled over to his former position by the starboard gunwale just forward of the tiller and dropped to the deck. Strangely, considering his avowed dislike of sea travel, he found the motion of the cutter unexpectedly comforting. Perhaps it was because, during his time on the water, he actually wouldn't be called upon to do anything. Whatever the reason, his eyelids began to droop, until a final thought struck him.

'*Captain* Payne,' he called out, with an unusual touch of banter. 'All I would ask of this voyage, is that we don't arrive at Sitka until night has fallen. The fewer people who are aware of Rodeen's presence, the better.'

Cleetus knew better than to bother asking why. All would no doubt become clear, so he merely flipped a casual salute and replied, 'Aye aye, *sir*. It will be my pleasure.'

Satisfied that he had done all that was necessary, Jake leaned back, closed his eyes, and within moments was fast asleep.

CHAPTER TWELVE

Three men moved quietly through the darkened streets towards the governor's residence atop Castle Hill. On their right shoulders, two of them carried a large and apparently heavy object, which, due to it being tightly wrapped in an oilskin tarpaulin, really could have been anything. Light flickered behind a number of shutters in cabins that had formerly been Russian owned, and raucous voices could be heard. Both male and female, they suggested that the US Army had nicely settled in.

The two sentries, posted at the mansion's main entrance, stamped their feet and kept close to the pitch-coated torch that flamed warmly. They had been on duty for hours, and thought only of their impending relief. It had quickly become apparent to all those on guard duty that nothing ever happened on Castle Hill at night, and so it was with some alarm that they heard the tramp of feet.

Clutching his regulation issue Springfield rifled musket, one of the soldiers nervously called out the standard challenge. 'Who goes there?'

Jake stepped to the fore. 'The name's Pierce. Jake Pierce. We need to see the colonel... now!'

'It's late,' the other sentry responded firmly. 'He won't thank us for disturbing him.'

The scout brushed the Springfield aside and advanced until he was almost nose to nose with the sentry. His features were haggard, his expression grim, and his voice dripped with menace. 'If you *don't* disturb him, I'll see you end up in the guardhouse for the rest of your life. You know damn well who we are. The colonel sent us out after Major Thomas's killer, and we've got one of them trussed up and ready to answer for his crimes.'

Both sentries stared at the bundle in stunned surprise. Then they glanced searchingly at each other. One of them nodded. Turning away, he opened one of the heavy double doors and disappeared inside.

Long minutes passed, and then quite abruptly there was a burst of activity. Both of the doors were flung open and Colonel Davis himself appeared. He held a large cigar and his face was flushed, as though the enlisted men in town weren't the only ones drinking that night. He glanced at the three civilians, before staring long and hard at their 'prisoner'.

'Am I to understand that you have a captive trussed up in there? Because if so, that is barbaric behaviour!'

Jake shrugged and immediately regretted it as a spasm of pain swept through his left arm. 'Needs must, colonel. An' happen you were to invite us in, I'd be able to give you a full explanation. Just you,

140

mind. For that report that you'll be *needing* to send to San Francisco.'

Recollection of his duty relating to the two slain officers brought Davis to his senses. 'Yes. Yes. The killings, of course. Follow me.' And then to the sentries, 'You men, shut these doors, and don't allow anyone else in.'

Moments later, Cleetus and Toby lowered their burden to the floor of Davis's expansive office, and untied the cords around the tarpaulin. Then the covering was pulled clear, and light from the various kerosene lamps illuminated Rodeen's bloody corpse in all its glory. The colonel stared at it in stunned amazement, and was momentarily lost for words.

'He don't look too good,' Toby drolly remarked.

'If you ask me, he looks too damn good, and he needs to stay that way for a spell longer,' Jake retorted.

Then Davis found his voice. 'What's the meaning of this, Pierce? Explain yourself.'

That man gave him a weary smile, and without asking permission eased his aching body into a chair. 'This is one of the two men that kilt Major Thomas and Lieutenant Curtis. The other lies dead in a stockade on the mainland. Except that they weren't really out to kill the officers.'

Davis blinked rapidly. He was beginning to regret having had that last drink or three. To give him time to think, he stared pointedly at Jake's arm. 'You're wounded. I should summon the surgeon.'

The scout shook his head. 'My arm can wait. Is Sergeant Beck still in the sickbay?'

141

'Beck. What's he got to do with anything?'

'That's what I must ask myself.'

The colonel frowned at the cryptic reply. He didn't normally concern himself with the whereabouts of his non-coms. 'I presume he's on light duties. And I'll ask you again. What is Beck to you?'

'Your officers were kilt because of something he'd done. He was the real target, if only by chance. But the only proof I've got is this stiff.'

Davis's eyes bulged. 'What possible use to us is a corpse?'

Jake chuckled and then winced. 'You'd be surprised what uses a dead body can have in trade. But it's not the teeth or hair I'm interested in. I'll just settle for its presence in daylight. An' from where I'm sitting I reckon we got it back just short of too late. So until reveille, I'd be obliged if you'd allow us to stay here. An' no one else must know that this cuss is dead.'

Cleetus had so far remained silent, but not any longer. 'An' for me there's the question of payment, colonel. I done what you asked, an' because of it one of my men died out there, on the Inside Passage. That wasn't part of our agreement.'

Davis regarded the big trader with distaste. 'All in good time, Mister Payne. I'm the Governor of Alaska, not a paymaster. Your account will be settled tomorrow, when my staff are on duty.'

Cleetus muttered something under his breath, but let the matter lie. Such a wait wasn't unreasonable, and besides he did want to see how things panned out with the mysterious Sergeant Beck. Then Jake's next words banished any thoughts of blood money from his mind, at least temporarily.

'How's about sharing your bottle with us, colonel? Seems to me like we've all earned a slug of "oh be joyful". After all, whatever else happens, Cleetus and me did catch your two assassins!' Then something else came to mind. 'Oh, and in a cellar in that stockade we found enough whiskey and weapons to put you in a very good light with General Halleck. But if you intend recovering them, best send a big detachment, because someone's really stirred up the Indians!'

*

Sergeant Josiah Beck had heard the rumours, but he found them hard to believe. That the hard-faced civilian scout had turned up out of nowhere, wounded and in the middle of the night with a prisoner bound up in a tarpaulin. He reckoned the sentries had imbibed a mite too much bug juice. But then he received the colonel's summons, and his guts began to churn unpleasantly. What if there was some truth in the scuttlebutt? What if Davis did have Rodeen or Teague up on Castle Hill, singing their story like a Western Meadowlark in the forest?

For a few frantic moments, the sergeant seriously considered making a run for it... before common sense prevailed. He was on an island, for God's sake, and stealing a boat wasn't an option, because he had no idea how to sail it or where to go. Or even what to do if he got there. Far better to face any accusers and deny everything. After all, it wasn't him who had slaughtered the two officers, and really that should be all that concerned the colonel. Recollection of that grim occurrence had him flexing his left hand. The arm was still bandaged and still sore, but it would serve.

Buckling on his belt with its regulation flap holster and cartridge box, Beck suddenly paused. He could be in need of an edge. Glancing over at his kit bag, he came to a decision. Unfastening it, he reached in and withdrew another Colt Army revolver that he had appropriated some years earlier. Such things were surprisingly easy to do, if a non-com possessed both cunning and opportunity. Reaching round, he lifted the back of his tunic and stuffed the gun, muzzle first, inside the belt of his trousers. Then he left his small log cabin, sucked in a deep draught of the chill morning air and strode purposefully towards Castle Hill.

*

That Jake Pierce possessed a steely resolve had never been in doubt, but that morning it was being severely tested. He really should have been in the care of the army surgeon. As it was, only a mixture of strong coffee and the colonel's personal supply of quality whiskey was keeping him on his feet. Knowing from which direction Beck would be approaching, Jake had stationed himself at the side of a cabin opposite the start of the gradient up to Castle Hill. In his right hand he held his Remington revolver, which was pretty much the only firearm he was capable of handling.

Looking up at the low wall surrounding the parade ground in front of the governor's mansion, he couldn't resist a smile. Standing next to one of the big guns, apparently in the best of health, was the figure of Clay Rodeen. That man's eyes were very much open, thanks to a liberal application of animal glue on the lids. Even more impressively, his right hand appeared to be pointing directly down at Jake's position, although that doubtless had something to do with Cleetus Payne, who was crouching behind and supporting the resurrected prisoner. At his side lay the trusty Spencer carbine that had served him so well on the mainland. Both men knew that this high risk scheme needed to work out better than the last time they had utilized a cadaver, back in the Tlingit encampment.

Conveniently for their purposes, the autumn sun shone from behind Rodeen's left shoulder, so that his waxy features were partly in shadow. Jake had refused Davis's offer of a military escort. He desired Beck's confession and arrest, rather than his demise, and feared that the sight of a squad of soldiers would merely encourage the non-com to flee. And so, with everything ready, all they had to do was wait. And not for long, as it turned out.

*

Josiah Beck strode boldly out from the cover of a clutch of log cabins and peered up the approach road to Castle Hill. The sun was partially in his eyes, and so he didn't immediately identify the lone figure apparently gazing down at him. But when recognition did finally come, his flesh turned colder than the Gulf of Alaska. So it was true. One of the bastards *had* returned unscathed.

'You'd be wise not to make any sudden moves, sergeant,' came a loud voice from somewhere behind him.

Beck uttered a long sigh, but otherwise remained motionless.

'Very sensible,' Jake continued. 'Now, with your left hand, unbuckle that gun belt and let it fall to the ground.'

'That arm don't work too well,' the non-com smoothly lied.

'Tough! It can't be any worse than mine. Take all the time you want, but do as I said or I'll drop this hammer.'

And so, without any apparent difficulty, Beck did as instructed.

'Now, slowly turn to face me.'

As his new captive complied, Jake relaxed slightly and lowered his revolver. He couldn't disguise the fact that he wasn't feeling too good, and even the handgun weighed heavy.

'Seems like we've both taken some lead recently,' the buck sergeant commented as he scrutinized the plainly weak army scout. He reckoned that, if pushed, he could easily overwhelm or elude him. Question was, who else did he have to contend with?

'Rodeen's told me everything,' Jake lied. 'Two good men died because of what you've been up to. So even though you didn't pull the triggers, you're gonna answer for your part in their murder.'

Behind his apparently calm demeanour Beck's mind was performing cartwheels. Gesturing back up the hill, he barked, 'You've only got that cockchafer's word for it.'

'It's enough for me, and more importantly, it's enough for the colonel,' Jake retorted, still with no knowledge of what 'it' was.

The soldier's eyes narrowed, as he appeared to reach a decision. 'Him and that poxy Teague had no idea I was even in Sitka, nor me them. And if they'd paid me for the guns three years ago like they'd promised, then they'd have had nothing to worry about anyway. In fact I probably wouldn't even be still in this God-damn army. As it was, they out and out robbed me,' he added bitterly.

So that was it! And now it was Jake's turn for some mental acrobatics. Feeling a familiar anger building within him, he came to certain ugly conclusions. He didn't much hold with happenstances, but what if this was one that really had come home to torment him?

'Guns for Indians,' he snarled. 'They had to be. Which makes me wonder which uprisings they would have been used in. I'm guessing it was Sioux or Cheyenne or some such. And being it was three years ago could place you in Kansas or Colorado.' As he spoke, his eyes took on a gleam of pure malevolence.

Beck had the wit to recognize jeopardy, but was a little too slow on the uptake. 'Why are you doing this? You got the men that kilt Thomas. An' what's it matter if a few army rifles went missing? It ain't like the Union was short of them. There was a war on, for Christ sake!'

Despite the chill, sweat began to bead on Jake's forehead. 'Because my wife and two children were murdered by Indians armed with guns bought from white men.'

It was Beck's turn to begin sweating. This had suddenly become very personal and very dangerous. But he did have an ace up his sleeve... or rather behind his back. 'An' what if Rodeen was dead? Huh?' he persisted. 'You wouldn't have a witness then. It'd be your word against mine.'

Jake favoured him with an icy smile. 'Lucky for us he's still breathing then, ain't it? Because it means *you* won't be for much longer!'

At that instant, Josiah Beck realized that a possibly manageable situation had become irretrievable, and everything changed. It was no longer just a matter of avoiding the provost's stockade. His very survival was at stake. With his left hand he reached out, as though pleading for forgiveness. At the same time, his right hand snaked under the back of his tunic and came out holding his other Colt, cocked and ready.

Not at his best and caught by surprise, Jake instinctively stepped back into the cover of the nearest cabin wall rather than try for the first shot. He just made it as the muzzle flared. The heavy ball kicked jagged splinters from a log, causing him to retreat further.

Beck then glanced up at the figure behind the low stone wall. Amazingly, Rodeen hadn't moved, and the opportunity to eliminate the only witness against him was too strong to resist. Rapidly shifting his aim, the sergeant drew a bead on the trader's chest and fired. That he hit him was not in doubt, because the cockchafer's jacket jumped under the impact of the .44 calibre ball. But amazingly, Clay Rodeen barely flinched. Then a carbine barrel appeared over the wall next to him, and Beck knew he had to run. Scooping up the discarded gun belt, he took to his heels in the direction of the cathedral. Above and behind him, a shot crashed out, and lead kicked up dirt a few feet ahead. Then Jake's voice bellowed out.

'I'll let you into a little secret, you bastard. Rodeen's been dead for days!'

The non-com blinked with bewilderment, but that was the only sign that he'd heard, because his headlong rush never slowed. Fellow soldiers stared at him in amazement as he raced past, but he ignored them. He no longer possessed any kind of plan. His instinct told him to make for the largest building, which was the Orthodox Cathedral of St Michaels, and of course the source of his current predicament. There ought to be enough nooks and crannies in there for him to hide away, get his breath back, and try to work out what to do next.

*

Colonel Jefferson C. Davis had been standing behind Rodeen's corpse with Sergeant Major Stubbs. They had overheard everything and witnessed the rogue trader's 'death' at the hands of their fellow soldier. The military governor's mind raced as he tried to make sense of what had just taken place. One thing was for sure, if he was to be seen in a good light by his superiors then there had to be a satisfactory conclusion to all this. Satisfactory for the army and therefore for him. That and the recovery of a size-able cache of contraband from the mainland might just be enough to earn him a general's star. Now that would be something!

'Mister Payne. You will assist Pierce in apprehending Sergeant Beck. I want him back alive or *dead*. Do you understand?' He quickly waved away the other man's objections. 'You will be well paid for your assistance.' Glancing over the wall, he could see the injured scout shambling after the fugitive. 'You'd better hurry. He looks like he might need the help. I will send on a squad of enlisted men to support you, but they may be understandably reluctant to fire on one of their own.'

Cleetus stared at him for a moment before nodding his grudging acceptance. He had long since regretted ever offering his services to the colonel, but it was too late to back off now. One of his crew had died on the *Good Fortune* because of Beck's crooked past, and he had been through enough with Jake not to want to see him killed as well. Turning away, he set off at a fast run down the approach road to Castle Hill.

Davis turned to his senior non-com. 'Stolen guns, eh. Send a man for Captain Barnes. He can lead the pursuit. And then dig out Beck's service record. I want to know where he served before here. Move man!' As the sergeant major broke into an unaccustomed sprint, the colonel added, mostly to himself, 'God damn! What I wouldn't give for a telegraph station up here.'

*

Josiah Beck heaved open one of the double doors and cursed fluently. An unexpected sea of faces stared back at him. It had never occurred to him that many of those evicted from their cabins would still be using the House of God as a temporary home. The cathedral's interior was strewn with hastily recovered bedding and personal possessions. As the wild-eyed, gun-toting sergeant burst in, those Russians and Tlingit nearest the entrance instinctively backed away, their fear very evident. Then it came to him that their numbers might be useful in hindering the inevitable pursuit. Swiftly thrusting the revolver back under his tunic, he buckled on his gun belt and then raised both arms in a sign of peace.

Deeply suspicious, but with nowhere else to go, the inhabitants sullenly shuffled aside as Beck made his way along the nave towards the bell tower. To his fevered mind that somehow seemed like the best place to go. Swiftly he mounted the winding stairs until, breathing hard, he reached the top. Surprisingly, the ornate bells had not been taken by the departing Russian élite, and were still in place. Looking out of one of the unglazed windows, he caught a glimpse of Jake Pierce hurrying down the street, and cursed his lack of a long gun, but decided to take a shot anyway.

Jake's heart was thumping, and his arm throbbed like the devil, but he was not so far gone as to miss the revolver that suddenly poked out over the sill. Rapidly he lurched to one side as it fired, although in truth the ball came nowhere near him.

'You're gonna have to do way better than that, Beck,' he yelled.

By way of reply, another cloud of smoke appeared in front of the tower and the second ball slammed into nearby timber. That one had been closer, but at such range it would take a deal of luck to improve on it. Being also armed with only a belt gun, meant that there was little point in responding, but then a crash from across the street indicated that the balance of power was changing. Cleetus had arrived with both his Spencer and Jake's Remington.

'Keep his head down while I get into the building,' the scout commanded.

'Okay. But don't even think about torching a cathedral, or there'll be more than just that sergeant out to kill you,' Cleetus advised. 'When the soldier boys get here, I'll set them to keeping his head down and follow you in there.' And with that he loosed off another shot at the tower.

'Yeah, yeah,' Jake retorted, before making a dash for the double doors. He wouldn't have cared to admit it, but he was glad to have the big trader at his back.

Encouragingly, no more gunfire came from above. And knowing where his prey was meant that he had no concerns about entering the building. Easing open the door, he stepped inside and let his eyes adjust to the weaker light. He too was surprised at the sight that greeted him. Yet because he wasn't wearing a uniform, and was therefore not regarded as an authority figure, the civilians displayed less fear at his arrival. One of them, a surprisingly young Russian seal hunter, smiled nervously at him, before pointing across the nave towards the stairs.

Nodding his thanks, he quickly moved to the foot of the bell tower. Stairs spiralled up to the tower. Common sense should have told him to wait. Beck had nowhere to go. All Jake had to do was stand fast until the others joined him, but he was beyond considering such things.

CHAPTER THIRTEEN

It was only now that he was pinned down below window level by rifle fire that Josiah Beck recognized that he was almost certain to die in the God-damned tower. And all because that thieving bastard Rodeen had cheated him out of a few guns and then mistakenly thought that the soldier had deliberately tracked him down. He glanced around his exposed 'redoubt' and cursed the lack of a trapdoor. Such a thing would definitely have aided his defence. Drawing the fully charged Colt from its holster, he retracted the hammer and placed it on the floor. The hideout gun only had two chambers remaining, and so he began to recharge the others by laboriously loading powder and ball from the muzzle end of the cylinder. Ominously, as he crammed in the charges with the integral rammer, he heard the wooden stairs creak. The only good thing about that was that they'd obviously decided not to burn him out. Well, more fool them, because he sure wasn't going under without a fight!

*

'Doesn't seem right, shooting at one of our own men,' Captain Barnes remarked as he dubiously surveyed the cathedral. The ten enlisted men that accompanied him hadn't even unslung their rifles.

Cleetus regarded him askance. 'It does if the pus weasel had something to do with the killings in there. Besides, all your men need to do is keep him busy. They ain't likely to score any kill shots from out here. I'm the one that's going in to help Jake.' It was an indication of how far their relationship had altered, in that he was now actually eager to do so. 'An' *you* need to make a move,' he prompted. 'Unless you want the colonel on your back.'

Barnes took the hint and soon his men were noisily blowing chunks of wood off the curving side of the tower. 'Keep at it,' Cleetus barked as he hurried off to the cathedral's double doors, a long gun slung over each shoulder. He sincerely hoped that Jake wouldn't attempt anything rash until he joined him.

*

'I'm coming for you, you son of a bitch!' Jake yelled up the stairs.

'You ain't got the *cojones* to take me on,' Beck retorted, deliberately hoping to needle the scout into something reckless while he was still alone.

155

Then the rate of fire in the street suddenly increased, and the sergeant found himself showered with splinters from the disintegrating window surrounds. Cursing, he crawled to the hatch and glanced down. There was a loud report and a ball flew past his left ear like a bee in flight. He jerked back. That had been way too close. His pursuer had to be far enough up the spiral stairs to have him in direct sight, which of course worked both ways.

Thrusting his revolvers over the edge, Beck fired simultaneously. The double crash reverberated painfully in the semi-enclosed space, and a cloud of smoke immediately obscured the stairs. Again cocking both weapons, he listened intently for any sounds of distress, but with projectiles still striking the outside of the tower his efforts were wasted. 'What the hell, it's worth a couple more,' he muttered.

Yet just as he once more pointed his Colts into the void, something totally unanticipated occurred. There was a tremendous clang as a piece of lead slammed into the underside of one of the bells hanging from a crossbeam above him. The misshapen metal then ricocheted down into the side of his face, carving a deep, bloody furrow through his left cheek. By a nasty twist of fate, the ball had come from one of his fellow soldiers, and the pain it caused was enough to draw a high-pitched scream from his lips.

A short distance below Beck's platform, Jake heard the two distinct noises, and resolved that he had to take his chance. Both of his opponent's shots had been too close for comfort, and he simply couldn't stay where he was. Desperately he mounted the stairs, but every step depleted his flagging reserves. He tried to steady himself against the single wooden rail with his left hand, but any effort with that arm brought forth fresh waves of agony. Finally his head went up through the hatch, and directly before him was Josiah Beck.

Sprawled on the floor, the bleeding non-com was quite obviously in a world of hurt. Then their tormented eyes met, and each of them acted instinctively. Jake swung his right arm up, levelled his revolver and squeezed the trigger. At that very instant, Beck kicked out with his booted left foot, deflecting the barrel just as it flared. The ball tore through the side of his boot, entirely removing his little toe in the process. Bizarrely, the original instrument of this destruction also sealed the wound, as the point-blank muzzle flash cauterised his raw flesh.

With a fresh wave of agony surging though him, Beck rolled away as though attempting to escape it. Thrown off balance by the kick, Jake had to drop the Colt so as to use his good arm for support. The gun scuttled off towards the side of the tower, temporarily out of reach. With a supreme effort, he finally staggered up on to the platform, and drew his Bowie.

'I'm gonna take you apart piece by piece,' he rasped, and flung himself at his foe.

In reaction to the torment that assailed him, Beck had also dropped one of his Colts, but he managed to swing the other round just in time and fired. The ball struck Jake full on in his chest, but the brutal impact wasn't enough to halt his precipitous descent. His body crashed down on to the sergeant, knocking all the wind from that man's lungs.

Desperate to take advantage of his momentary ascendancy, the scout attempted to plunge his cold steel into Beck's guts, but the long blade was tightly wedged in the flooring, and his right arm simply wouldn't respond. In fact he couldn't even lift his head. It was as though all his remaining strength had abruptly deserted him. With a supreme effort, the man beneath him heaved with both arms and tossed Jake's broken body aside.

Beck sucked in a deep breath, and with difficulty got to his knees. 'Brought a knife to a gunfight, huh?' he sneered scornfully. Then, with blood dripping from his chin, he cocked the Colt and pointed it directly at Jake's face. All that individual could do was stare helplessly up at the gaping muzzle.

A shot rang out, but its source was not the one that Beck had expected, and neither was the result. A bullet from his opponent's powerful 'buffalo gun' smashed into his skull, destroying it like a ripe melon, and showering the dying scout with blood and gore. Without uttering another sound, Sergeant Josiah Beck collapsed on to the timber floor and lay still.

Cleetus Payne cautiously entered the tower with Jake's smoking Remington rolling block rifle and, nearly doubled over, approached a window. 'Hold fire, you damn fools,' he bellowed into the street. 'The job's done.' After waiting a few moments, he added, 'You hear me, captain?'

'I hear you, *Mister* Payne,' came the clipped response, and sure enough all shooting ceased.

Only then did Cleetus stand tall and turn his attention to the appalling carnage before him. Beck was undoubtedly finished, and although it grieved him to admit it, his companion appeared to be too. 'Why the hell didn't you wait for me?' he mournfully enquired. 'We could have taken him on together.'

Jake Pierce, his coat now soaked with blood, peered up at him and smiled weakly. 'I can't abide tardiness,' he softly replied. Then, as his eyelids slowly closed, his head lolled to one side, and a man with more blood on his hands than an army surgeon at Shiloh quietly passed away.

Cleetus stared long and hard at the dead army scout. Though a few days earlier he would never have thought it possible, tears began to trickle down his hairy face. Jake had undoubtedly been a hard and embittered individual, but he hadn't been all bad. The big trader still didn't fully understand what it had all been about, and now he supposed it no longer mattered, anyway. Davis would send off his self-serving report, and that would be an end of it. Suddenly strangely mindful of where he was, Cleetus sketched the sign of a cross, which was definitely a first for him. There *was* one thing he could be certain about. Here lay a real *hombre*, and he intended to make damn sure that the new owners of Sitka realized it!